TANK & FIZZ

THE CASE OF THE BATTLING BOTS

TANK & FIZZ

THE CASE OF THE BATTLING BOTS

BY

LIAM O'DONNELL

ILLUSTRATED BY

MIKE DEAS

ORCA BOOK PUBLISHERS

Library and Archives Canada Cataloguing in Publication

O'Donnell, Liam, 1970–, author
The case of the battling bots / Liam O'Donnell; illustrated by Mike Deas.
(Tank & Fizz)

Issued in print and electronic formats.
ISBN 978-1-4598-0813-3 (paperback).—ISBN 978-1-4598-0814-0 (pdf).—
ISBN 978-1-4598-0815-7 (epub)

1. Graphic novels. I. Deas, Mike, 1982-, illustrator II. Title.
III. Title: Tank and Fizz.
PS8579.D646C38 2016   jC813'.6   C2015-904488-x
C2015-904489-8

First published in the United States, 2016
Library of Congress Control Number: 2015946327

Summary: In this illustrated middle-grade novel and second book in the Tank and Fizz series,
a goblin detective and a technology-tinkering troll must dodge battle bots and spellbooks to
prevent the return of an ancient demon.

MIX
Paper from
responsible sources
FSC® C016245

*Orca Book Publishers is dedicated to preserving the environment and
has printed this book on Forest Stewardship Council® certified paper.*

Orca Book Publishers gratefully acknowledges the support for its publishing
programs provided by the following agencies: the Government of Canada through
the Canada Book Fund and the Canada Council for the Arts, and the Province of British
Columbia through the BC Arts Council and the Book Publishing Tax Credit.

Design by Jenn Playford
Illustrations and cover image by Mike Deas

ORCA BOOK PUBLISHERS
www.orcabook.com

Printed and bound in Canada.

19 18 17 16 • 4 3 2 1

To goblin detectives and
troll tinkerers everywhere.
—Liam O'Donnell

To Justin and Kaylee
—Mike Deas

CHAPTER ONE

Bot Attack!

The robot was going to crush me.

I froze like a midwinter booger on a bike rack. The battle bot stomped closer with its massive feet. The ground shook with every step. It reached out with its long arms. Its sharp claws were perfect for crushing other bots. And smushing goblin detectives like me.

The name is Marlow. Fizz Marlow. Fourth-grade goblin, part-time detective and reluctant battle-bot bait.

It wasn't my idea to step into the arena with the Rawlins Reaper, the toughest battle bot at Gravelmuck Elementary.

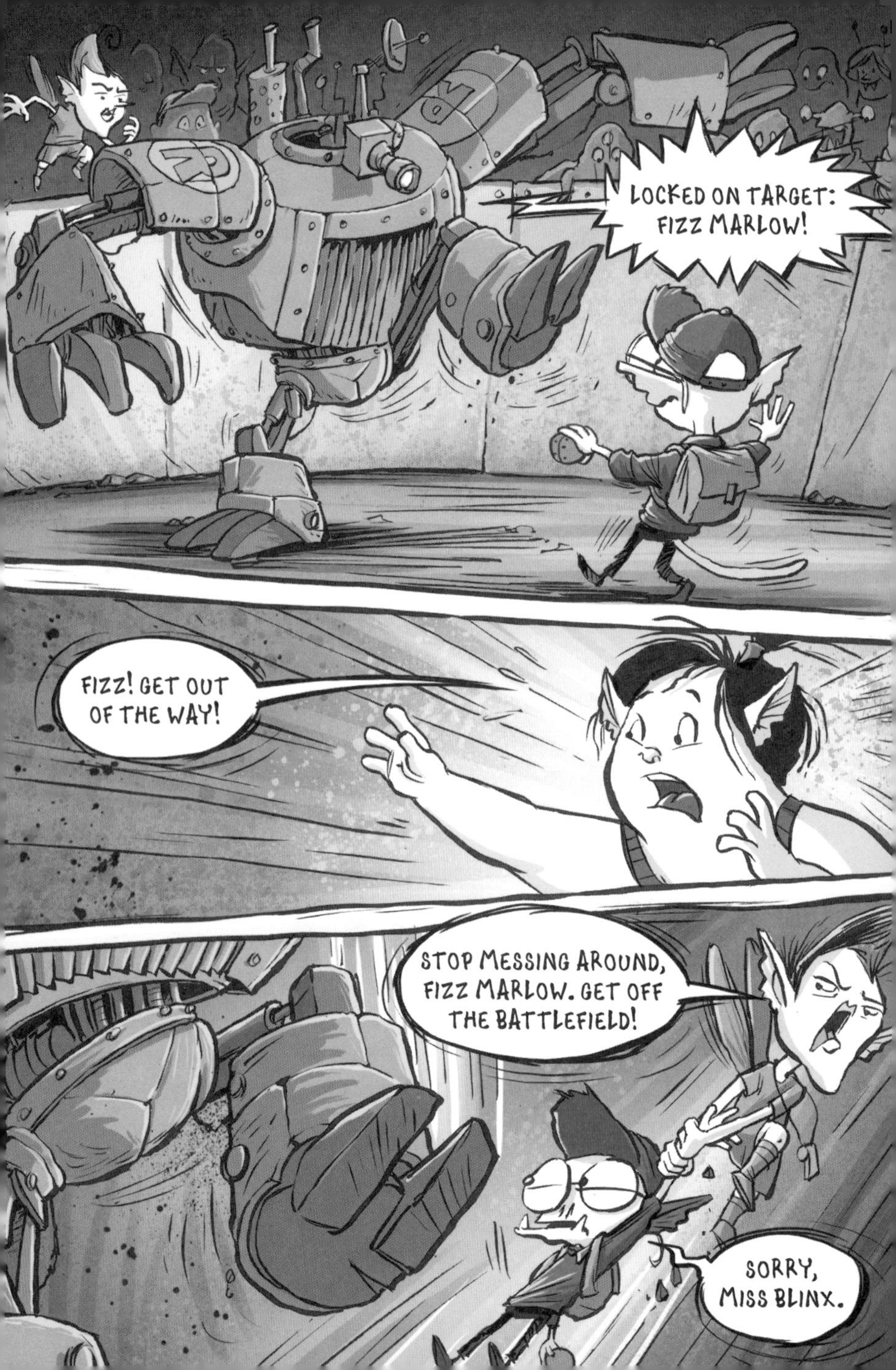
LOCKED ON TARGET: FIZZ MARLOW!
FIZZ! GET OUT OF THE WAY!
STOP MESSING AROUND, FIZZ MARLOW. GET OFF THE BATTLEFIELD!
SORRY, MISS BLINX.

I'LL GET YOU NEXT TIME, MARLOW!

SLAM!

Miss Blinx dropped me on my tail. Tank Wrenchlin, my best friend and detective partner, lifted me to my feet.

"That was close," she said. "Rizzo's battle bot could have smushed you!"

"You said I needed to get close!" I said.

"There's close and then there's *too* close, Fizz."

"Well, I'm not getting that close to Rizzo's battle bot ever again." I handed her the small metal ball she had given me only a few minutes ago. "You can take your code smeller back."

"It's a code *sniffer*, Fizz." Tank was the best troll tinkerer this side of the Dark Depths. Inside the ball were gears, circuits and a bunch of other stuff I didn't understand. But Tank did, and that was all that mattered.

She inspected the ball for damage. "And I didn't tell you to nearly get stuck to the battle bot's foot. We're trying to solve a case, not turn you into goblin pancakes."

Solving a case was the reason I'd gotten into that battle in the first place. No one ever said being a detective would be easy. I just wished they would remind me to wear a helmet once in a while.

The whole mess had started two days earlier, when the Troll Patrol cornered us on our way home from school. Thankfully, they didn't patrol for unfinished homework, or I would have been rounded up a lot earlier. The three grade-eight trolls were Gravelmuck Elementary's champion battle-bot team. They were also our school's best chance at winning this year's Battle Bot Cup. That is, if everyone played fairly.

"Rizzo Rawlins is a cheat," said the tallest of the three trolls. His name was Daztan. He was the Troll Patrol captain.

"And the Tuesday lunch special is a health hazard," I said. "Tell us something we don't know, Daztan."

I'm normally not so snarky to older monsters. But I had a serious video-game session and a fresh batch of choco-slug cookies waiting for me at home. It's never a good idea to get between me and my video games.

"Rizzo Rawlins has put together his own battle-bot team to compete in the school finals," said Ryla, the smallest of the three trolls. She was the coder of the group. It was her computer code that made the Troll Patrol's battle bots the best in the school.

"But Rizzo is only in fourth grade," Tank said. "How can he compete with you older monsters?"

"Rizzo gets whatever Rizzo wants," said Zarkof. He was smaller than Daztan but larger than Ryla, and had bright-orange hair spiked up to look like he'd been electrocuted. "Rizzo convinced Principal Weaver to let him compete, and then he hired some of the other kids in our class to build him a battle bot."

"Normally, we would be able to defeat any bot they could scrape together," Daztan said.

"We've watched his bot in battle," Zarkof said. "We think he is cheating."

"Word on the playground is that you two are detectives," said Zarkof.

"Best in the school," Tank said with a smile.

"Good," Daztan said. "We want to hire you."

Thoughts of cookies and video games vanished from my detective brain. I was always interested in a new case. But still, I had my doubts.

"Everyone knows Rizzo Rawlins is a cheat," I said. "How can we prove he's cheating in the battle-bot competition?"

The flat piece of vizpaper in Zarkof's large hands sparked to life. The paper's surface glowed softly with the words *Rockfall Battle Bot Association: Rules and Regulations*. Zarkof thumbed through the manual. He cleared his throat before speaking.

"It states clearly in Section 12, Subsection D, that all essential mainframe apparatuses and sub-linear underlying frameworks must be—"

"Um, run that one by me again," I said.

"Certainly." Zarkof smiled. "It states clearly in Section 12—"

Daztan stepped in to translate. "What he means is, we have to build our battle bots using parts we make ourselves."

"And run the bots using computer code that we write ourselves," Ryla added. "That way, participants can't just buy the best equipment or hire some professional computer coder to make their battle bot."

"And that's what you think Rizzo has done?"

Daztan nodded. "His bot moves too fast. It's too smart to have been created by a bunch of monsters from elementary school. We think he got his battle-bot parts and code from a professional bot maker. And we want *you* to prove it."

"It is quite important that the truth be known," Zarkof said. "The winner of our school battle-bot tournament will represent Gravelmuck in the Slick City Battle Bot Cup next week."

"And you think Rizzo will win?" Tank asked.

"If he does win, he won't deserve it," Ryla said.

"We just want things to be fair," Daztan said. "All the other monsters have been working on their battle bots for a long time. It's not right for Rizzo to use his money to get an advantage over us."

"If you can prove he bought his computer parts, Principal Weaver will have to remove him from the tournament."

"A chance to prove Rizzo Rawlins is a cheat?" I looked to my detective partner. Tank's ears stood at attention like a pair of hungry flame hounds. She was in.

WE'LL TAKE THE CASE!

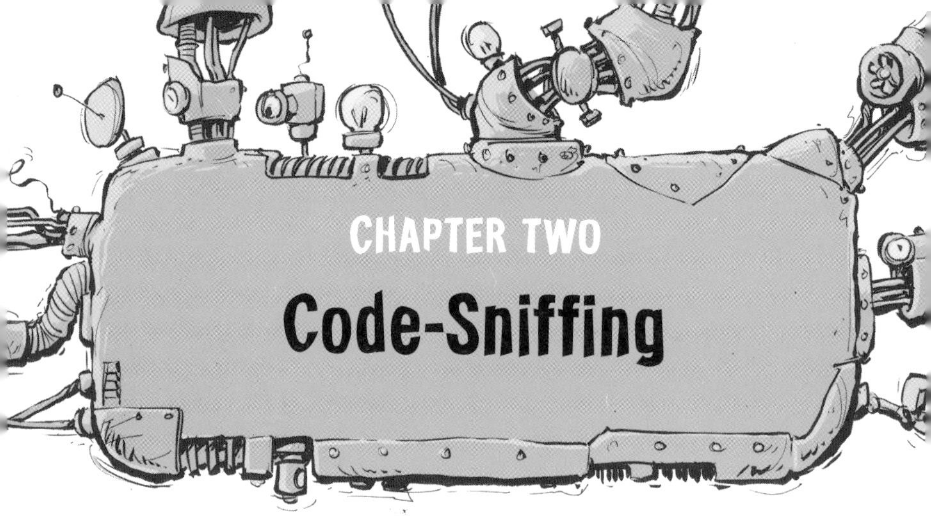

CHAPTER TWO

Code-Sniffing

Two days later, Tank's ears had started to sag.

Rizzo and his crew weren't letting anyone near their battle bot. The kobold wouldn't talk to me or Tank. Even Rizzo's goons, the Gutro twins, were keeping tight-lipped about what made the Rawlins Reaper work.

When the Gravelmuck battle-bot finals rolled around, it was a match between Rizzo's Reaper and the Troll Patrol Thrasher.

After chasing that kobold for two days, we had nothing. Now the whole school had gathered in the schoolyard to see the battle. Rizzo's dad, Ratso Rawlins, had even rented a special battle-bot arena with seats for the fans.

I had dusted myself off from the close encounter with Rizzo's battle bot and was ready to never get in the ring again. Tank had other ideas.

"Luckily, you didn't damage the code sniffer when you nearly got stomped. Let's keep it that way." Tank handed me the small copper ball again. "I was up all last night building this thing. It will detect all the computer code running around here."

A tiny seam ran around the circumference of the metal. The seam was split on one side by a small screen. A blue light pulsed on the screen like a heartbeat.

"Every coder signs his computer code. If the sniffer detects code that is not signed by any members of Rizzo's team, it will flash red."

"And that will prove Rizzo is using code he didn't write."

"Exactly," Tank said. "And that should be enough to prove he's cheating."

A shadow fell across the Troll Patrol work area. We all looked up to see a giant spider hanging over us from a long thread of web silk. Principal Weaver.

"Attention! Attention! Your attention, please!" The spider barked through her megaphone as if we were on the other side of Slick City and not just a tail's length away. "I wish the Troll Patrol the best of luck. You'll need it against Rizzo Rawlins and his brilliant battle bot!"

Principal Weaver swung across the arena to sit near Rizzo's team before the trolls could say anything.

"No prizes for guessing who she wants to win," Ryla muttered.

"Don't sweat it," I said. "Principal Weaver just wants to keep Rizzo happy so his dad will keep giving the school money."

Miss Blinx buzzed to the center of the battle-bot field.

"All right, monsters!" she shouted. She might be the size of an ogre's finger, but that blaze fairy didn't need a megaphone to be heard. "Let's get ready to rumble!"

The battle bots lumbered into the arena. The battle began with a loud cheer from the monsters in the bleachers.

I slipped into the crowd and away from the bot action. I was sad to be missing the battle, but I had a cheating kobold to catch.

I pushed through a group of latecomers hurrying to their seats. All the classes had been let out for the afternoon to see the final. It looked like every parent in the neighborhood had taken the day off work too.

Tank's code sniffer felt cool and solid in my hand. Its light wasn't on. I was tempted to shake the thing to see if it was actually working. I should know better. When my pal Tank builds something, it works. Every time. Well, almost every time. There was that incident with the sizzlematic portable grubnug-fudge maker. It made grubnug fudge, all right. Enough to fill my room all the way up to my window. It took me a week to clean up, and the whole apartment smelled of fudge for a month. Mom banned Tank from bringing her inventions over to our place. It was a delicious cleanup though.

I made my way to Rizzo's tech pit. His battle-bot crew had their backs to me. They were too busy watching the fight to see me coming. Rizzo stood on the edge of the arena with the bot controller in his paws. He yelped and barked as he controlled the battle bot in the middle of the arena.

I moved past a crate spilling over with wires and electronics to get a closer look at the action.

The Rawlins Reaper moved faster than a first-grader riding a sugar rush. It zipped around the Troll Patrol Thrasher, scoring direct hits almost every time. The Thrasher didn't know where to swing its mighty claws. On the far side of the ring, Ryla struggled at the controls of the Thrasher. Rizzo had come out swinging, and he wasn't going to stop.

I checked Tank's code sniffer. It was in pulse over-load, flashing red like it was going to explode.

Julius and Seymor Gutro were Rizzo's go-to goons. They were on me like stink on a sneaker.

"Get back here, Fizzle!" Seymor shouted.

"We just want to talk," added his brother. Yeah right. Those two talked with their fists. I raced out of the tech pit. Julius and Seymor were one ogre-sized step behind me.

Tank's copper ball glowed in my hands. Now that it was farther away from Rizzo and the illegal code running his battle bot, it had stopped flashing red. That wasn't stopping his goons from chasing me.

I scrambled up to the top of the bleachers. The seats were packed with cheering battle-bot fans. I slipped behind the last row of seats. No one took notice of me. They were all too busy watching the action down below.

THE TROLL PATROL THRASHER CAN'T KEEP UP WITH THE RAWLINS REAPER!

RIZZO'S ILLEGAL SOFTWARE IS MAKING HIS BOT TOO FAST AND STRONG! THE TROLLS CAN'T WIN.

The Gutro brothers dangled me over the back of the bleachers like a mudcrawler on a hook. It was a long way down. Far enough to squish a little goblin like me.

Julius held out a meaty paw.

"Give us the glowing ball, Fizzle."

Seymor sneered. "Or we'll come looking for it, and we can't guarantee no bruises."

A loud crunch echoed up from the middle of the arena. A cheer erupted from the crowd. Somebody's robot had just gotten smacked. A sinking feeling in my gut told me it wasn't the Reaper.

I had a choice—get dropped like a goblin water balloon or roughed up by the school bullies. It wasn't much of a choice. And it was all over a flashing little ball that had already told me what I needed to know. Rizzo was running illegal code. He was cheating.

If the goons really wanted Tank's ball, they could have it. I held out the code sniffer.

"Here you are, fellas."

The Gutro brothers grinned.

"Now he knows who's running the show," said Julius.

"We just had to shake him up a bit," Seymor said.

All they had to do was take the ball from me. Simple, right? But there's nothing these two can't mess up.

Seymor decided to prove his point. He gave me a shake I wasn't expecting.

The copper ball slipped from my fingers.

All three of us watched the code sniffer drop to the crowd below. It landed on the back of a very large spider scuttling through the crowd. A spider we all knew.

"Principal Weaver!" Julius said.

Seymor's glare burned into me. "See what you've done, goblin! Now we'll never get that ball."

"You're the one that shook me!" I said. "And you're the one dangling me over the edge of the bleachers!"

Top tip—never remind an ogre he's dangling you over the back of the bleachers.

Seymor grinned. "How about we send you down there to get that ball back for us?"

"Yeah, we can get you down there real quick," Julius said. He made a noise that was halfway between a giggle and a snort.

Seymor loosened his grip on my collar. If I didn't think of something quick, I'd be taking a one-way trip down onto my principal's head.

Another roar erupted behind us.

"And the winner is Rizzo Rawlins!" Miss Blinx's voice boomed over the cheering crowd.

Seymor spun to face the arena. I whizzed around with the big ogre and away from the back of the bleachers. In the middle of the arena, Rizzo's battle bot shuffled around in a jerky victory dance. The Thrasher had been thrashed. It lay on the ground in a crumpled heap.

I had missed the battle, but it was clear Rizzo's illegal code had helped him win.

Seymor jumped in the air and high-fived his brother. The combination of jumping and high-fiving was clearly too much for the ogre's tiny brain. His left hand forgot what his right hand was doing. He let me go. I crashed onto the bleachers and scrambled away before the big lug realized what he'd done. At the speed his brain worked, I probably had a week or two's head start, but I wasn't taking any chances.

I raced down the bleachers and headed to the Troll Patrol's tech pit. There would be tears and anger at losing the battle-bot finals. But I was doing a victory dance inside.

I had proof that Rizzo had cheated. That proof was now riding on the back of my principal. If I could get my hands on the code sniffer, justice would be served to that dog-faced bully.

CHAPTER THREE
Principals & Press Conferences

The door to Principal Weaver's office loomed over us like an end-of-the-year report card.

"Are you sure this is a good idea?" Tank said.

"This is a terrible idea," I said. "But it's the only one we have."

We had argued all night about this plan. After Rizzo's victory in the battle-bot arena the day before, we'd joined the Troll Patrol at the Bouncing Bugbear Café, where they were drowning their sorrows with double grubnug-fudge smoothies. There weren't enough smoothies in all of Rockfall Mountain to drown out the feeling that they had been robbed.

Before landing on Principal Weaver's sticky back, Tank's code sniffer had proved that Rizzo powered his battle bot with illegal code. He'd cheated. And he'd won. We needed to get the sniffer back from Weaver or the Rawlins Reaper would be going to the Slick City Battle Bot Cup at the brand-new Slurp Stadium next week. Our clients, the Troll Patrol, deserved to go to the finals. It wasn't right. It was also personal.

All year, I had watched Rizzo cheat in class. Math tests, science quizzes, coloring contests. You name it, Rizzo Rawlins cheated. He bribed the school math whizzes for test answers. His goons sabotaged classmates' experiments. He hired professional artists to do his cut-and-paste craft projects. Rizzo Rawlins had to win at everything, every time, any way he could.

I had seen the trail of broken dreams in my school-mates' tears. When I'd seen the sad faces of the Troll Patrol, I knew Rizzo's cheating had to stop. And I was the goblin to make that happen.

The only monster who could stop Rizzo was on the other side of that door. Principal Weaver. She was the meanest principal on this side of the Dark Depths. When you got in trouble, she didn't put you in detention—she put you on the menu. Her policy was "three strikes and you're lunch." Last year, Zazzie Malawar, a troll in the fifth grade, got into trouble three times in one month. He went into Weaver's office and was never seen again. Some say his family moved away. Others say he became a troll burrito for Principal Weaver and her army of spider babies. That was one mystery I was not willing to solve.

"We can't stand here all day," Tank said.

"Don't rush me!" I snapped.

The doors swung open. A thick strand of web silk shot out from the darkness and smacked into my chest. Another strand stuck to Tank's chest. The strands yanked us through the doorway and into the darkness.

So much for not being rushed.

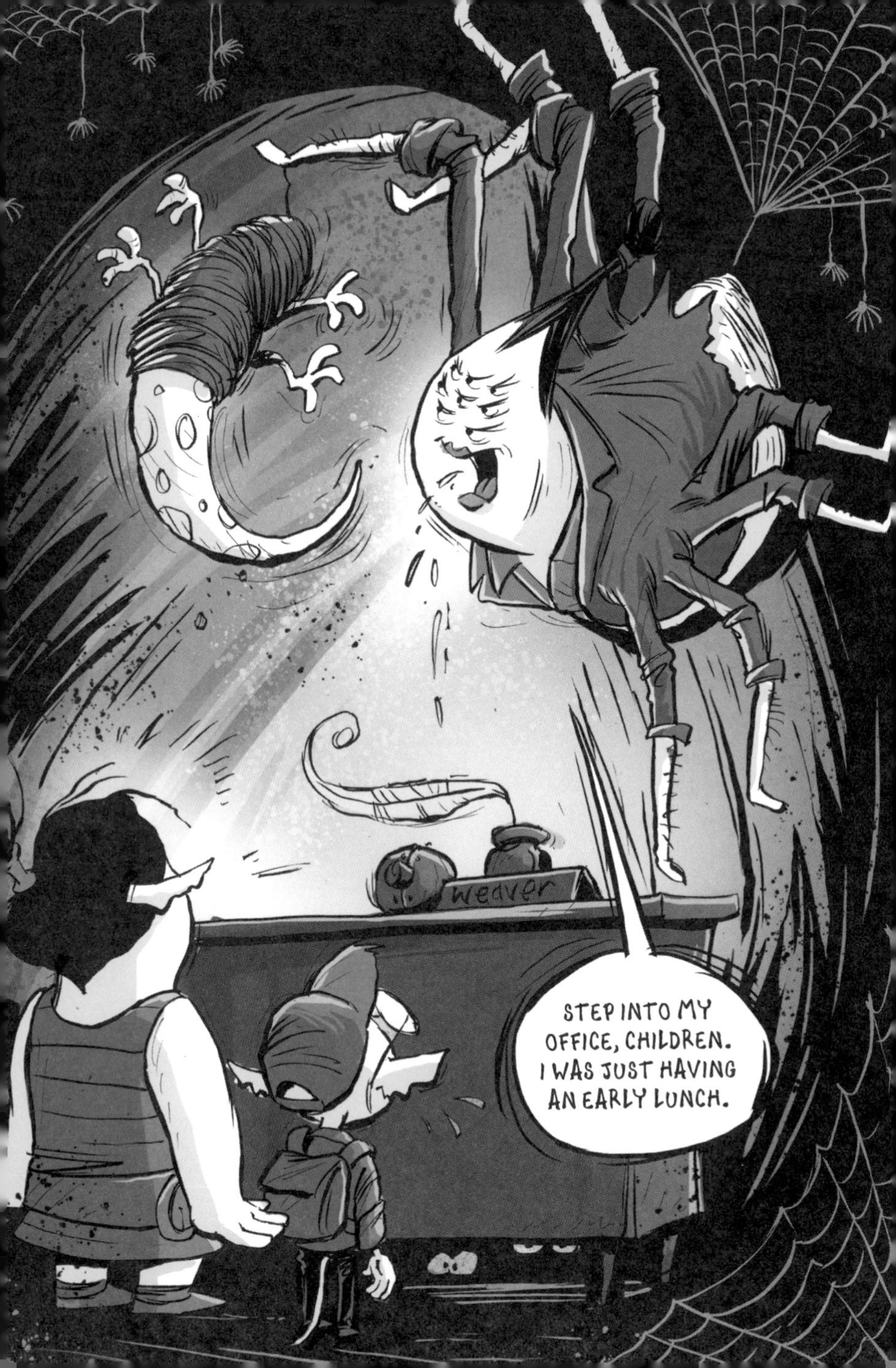
weaver
STEP INTO MY OFFICE, CHILDREN. I WAS JUST HAVING AN EARLY LUNCH.

Principal Weaver's eight eyes peered at us through the gloom of her office. Sticky webs covered every surface.

Tiny shapes scuttled along the walls. Rustling legs scurried across the floor. Weaver's children. A baby spider crawled across my foot, sending a cold shiver along my tail. It pounced on something smaller in the dark and spun it into a sticky cocoon. Then it carried its prize back to the corner and disappeared into the wall of webs.

"Aren't they adorable?" Principal Weaver said. "Spinning their own webs! They grow up so fast, don't they?"

Weaver's spider babies were her eyes and ears around the school. Always lurking above. Always listening. Always watching. No doubt the spider babies told Principal Weaver we were just outside her door. But they couldn't tell her why we were here.

Thankfully, Tank could. My detective partner got straight to the point.

"Rizzo Rawlins is cheating," she said.

Principal Weaver swallowed the last bite of her snack.

"Rizzo? Never!" she said. She slid down her web and landed on her desk. Under the layer of webbing I spied the round shape of the code sniffer. "He's a model student. You could both learn a lot from him." The kids at Gravelmuck had already learned a lot from Rizzo. We had all learned what it feels like to be lied to, bullied and cheated. I was done learning from that kobold.

Rizzo Rawlins had everyone fooled, including Principal Weaver. Actually, it was the Rawlins family fortune that had Weaver fooled. Mr. Rawlins owned a bunch of stores across Rockfall Mountain. The Rawlinses had money. And they spent a lot of that money on the school. That money had also given Rizzo a lifetime of straight As and gold stars.

"Rizzo Rawlins and his family have been very good to this school," Principal Weaver said. "I won't have any bad words said about them."

Bad words were all I had. It was a good thing my throat felt like it was stuck shut with webs and no words could come out.

"It's the truth," Tank said. She stamped her foot. Well, she tried to, but it was stuck to the floor, so she ended up with more of a squish than a stamp. "Rizzo used computer code he didn't write to control his battle bot. That's why his bot was so fast on the battle-field. That's how he won the last battle!"

"The proof is right there on your desk." My words came out in a croak, but it was enough.

One of Weaver's legs tapped the web-coated code sniffer.

"This is yours?" Principal Weaver rubbed three legs along her backside. "You dented my abdomen dropping it on me like that."

"I didn't drop it," I said. "It was Julius and Seymor."

"Enough!" Weaver snapped. "I don't want to see this ridiculous contraption again."

She pushed the code sniffer off the desk. A pair of baby spiders scurried out. They climbed over the code sniffer like it was a tasty first-grader. Together, they rolled the ball into the shadows. Tank's whole body slumped as she watched all her hard work disappear forever.

"You are just sad your troll friends didn't win," Principal Weaver said. "You two should be ashamed of yourselves. Trying to blame poor Rizzo. He works hard, follows the rules and is nice to everyone at the school. Now get back to class before things get too sticky for you."

Webs splatted onto our backs. Two large spider babies hanging above the door reeled in the webs and dragged us out of the office. The door slammed in our faces.

The meeting was over. Rizzo was still battle-bot champion and still a cheat.

CHAPTER FOUR

Skateboards & Stakeouts

After school, Tank and I crouched in a glowshroom patch. Principal Weaver's words rang in my ears.

"How can that old spider not see Rizzo is a cheater?" I said.

"Because Rizzo's dad has paid for half the school," Tank said beside me. She kept her zoomers pressed to her eyes as she spoke.

"So that means his son gets to cheat his way into the Battle Bot Cup?"

"Not if we can help it," Tank said. "Now keep your voice down and quit squirming."

Squirming is what I do best when I'm crammed into a small space. Tank and I had followed Rizzo from school to his dad's warehouse. The kobold and the Gutro twins had gone in the back door about an hour ago. We had not seen them since. With Tank's code sniffer lost in Weaver's webs, we had to find more evidence to prove Rizzo was cheating. That called for a good old-fashioned detective stakeout. And that had brought us to this glowshroom patch. Stakeouts always left me with a cramp in my tail.

"Here he comes," Tank said.

WHERE IS HE GOING NOW?

HOP ON AND LET'S FIND OUT!

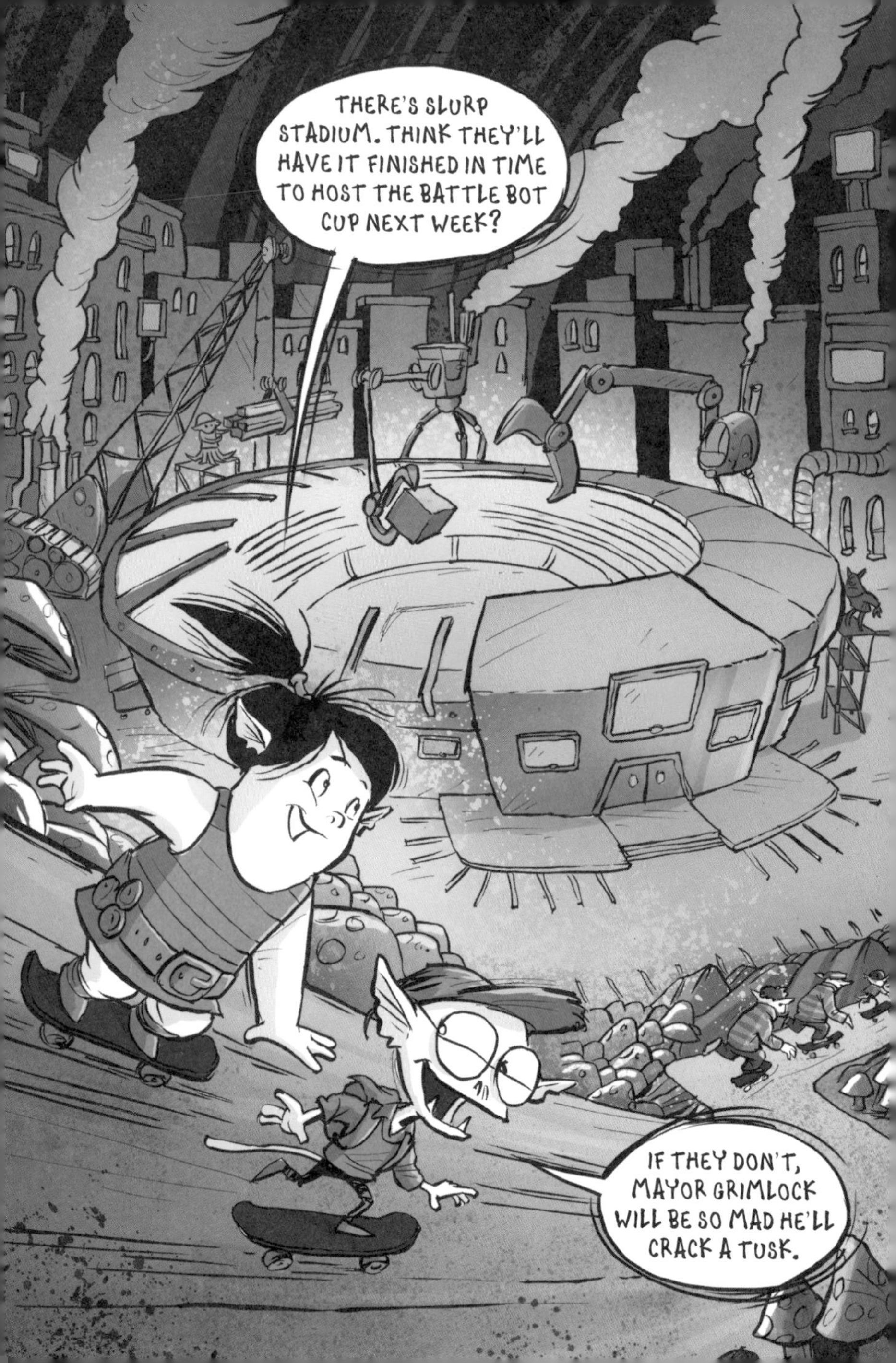
THERE'S SLURP STADIUM. THINK THEY'LL HAVE IT FINISHED IN TIME TO HOST THE BATTLE BOT CUP NEXT WEEK?
IF THEY DON'T, MAYOR GRIMLOCK WILL BE SO MAD HE'LL CRACK A TUSK.

Slurp Stadium was the newest addition to Slick City and Mayor Grimlock's pet project. The massive concrete arena dominated this part of town. It was almost finished. Metal scaffolding still stood in front of the far end of the stadium, and a small army of troll and goblin workers swarmed around the building. The construction workers all wore the same gray SlurpCo Industries coveralls and tired faces. They were working around the clock to add the final touches before the Battle Bot Cup.

The mayor had ignored complaints from local monsters who didn't want Slurp Stadium built. He'd even ordered a whole glowshroom grove torn down to make room for it. The stadium was named after its biggest sponsor, SlurpCo. The company owned half of Slick City and mined the goopy slick out of Fang Harbor. Slurp Stadium was supposed to be the best thing ever to happen to Slick City. Or the biggest disaster, depending on which monster you spoke to.

Rizzo and his goons rolled into the empty parking lot across from the stadium. Tank and I skated behind a dumpster that smelled of rotting haggle fish.

"We're not going to be able to see anything from here," I said.

"We won't have to," Tank said. She pulled a metal box out of her backpack. It had a propeller on one side. "This will be our eyes."

IT'S NOT ANOTHER CODE SNIFFER?

EVEN BETTER. A SPYBOT!

IT HAS A CAMERA.

"Yep, and it'll silently record everything," Tank said. She sent the bot buzzing into the air. "We just have to get it close to Rizzo without him spotting it."

"That plan didn't work out very well with your code sniffer."

"Yes, but this time *I'm* in charge, Fizz."

We crouched behind the smelly dumpster. Rizzo and his goons wouldn't be able to see us, but we could see them. We had ringside seats to whatever no-good Rizzo was up to.

The parking lot blurred on the screen of Tank's little phone. The mechanical bot focused on Rizzo and his goons.

"They're just standing there," I said. "Are they lost?"

"How can they be lost, Fizz?" Tank said, her eyes glued to the screen. Without looking up, she pointed off to her right. "Slurp Stadium is right there! I know it's new and all, but it's kind of hard to miss." The screen on the wall behind Rizzo buzzed loudly. It flashed, and the smiling face of the troll selling cavity-fighting fangpaste vanished. Another face appeared. I could tell from the sharp jaw and angry eyes that it was definitely not selling dental products.

Tank zoomed the camera closer on the face on the billboard.

"Your bug have sound?" I said.

"Sort of," Tank said. She tapped her phone screen. "I just rewired the microphones, but I haven't had a chance to test them."

She adjusted the controls on the screen. A low buzzing came through the phone's speakers. The buzzing turned to words.

"You did well, kobold," said the face on the ad.

"It worked out this time," Rizzo said. The phone's tiny speakers made it sound like he was trapped in a tin can. "But for the next round, we'll need something more."

The speakers went suddenly quiet.

"What happened?" I said.

"Mic failure on the bot," she said with a shrug. Tank tapped the controls on her phone. "I told you I haven't had time to test it out."

"Get the sound back!" I reached for the volume control. "What about pressing this button?"

Tank swatted my hand away.

"Hands off, Fizz! The controls are really touchy. Let me do the driving."

"I don't want to drive. I want to hear!"

"Just watch the screen," Tank said. "At least we can still see."

What we saw didn't make any sense. What was Rizzo up to? Why was he out here in an empty parking lot after school? Who was that weird mask on the screen on the wall? And since when could ads talk to monsters?

Whatever the mask was saying, Rizzo liked it. He jumped up and down and barked with glee.

At Rizzo's command, Julius and Seymor ran to the garbage bin beside them.

Tank flew her spybot closer. The little bot hovered just above Rizzo and the twins. They didn't even notice.

On-screen, we saw Julius rummaging through the garbage, tossing out empty coffee cups and food containers. He pulled out a small square of metal and held it up. It was the size of a lunch box. Wires sprouted from the box on all sides. Rows of lights ran along the edges.

"What is that?" I leaned in close to Tank's phone to get a better look.

"Get off me, Fizz." She pushed me back with one hand. "You're going to make me—"

THUNK!

We both froze.

Mangy fur filled the screen on Tank's phone. The image blurred, shook and then zoomed into focus on a pair of beady eyes and a long snout.

Rizzo stared back at us through the bot's camera.

"Fly away!" I hissed.

Tank tapped and swiped at the bot controls. "I can't," she said. "Rizzo grabbed the spybot. I can't get away."

Rizzo's toothy grin took up the entire screen. He dropped the bot to the ground. The last thing we saw was the bottom of Rizzo's boot stepping down hard. Then the screen went blank.

"Busted," I said.

"Literally. My spybot is trashed!" Tank said. "Thanks to you, Fizz."

There was no time for apologies.

I poked my head around the dumpster. Rizzo pointed in our direction.

"Get 'em, boys!" he shouted.

The Gutro brothers charged toward us on their skateboards.

"Here we go again," I said.

Tank hopped on her board and skated out of the parking lot.

Being chased by Rizzo's goons twice in one week was definitely a new record for me. I didn't want to add getting caught twice to my list of achievements. I hopped on my board and raced out of the parking lot too.

I caught up to Tank across the street. She rolled toward the looming shadow of Slurp Stadium.

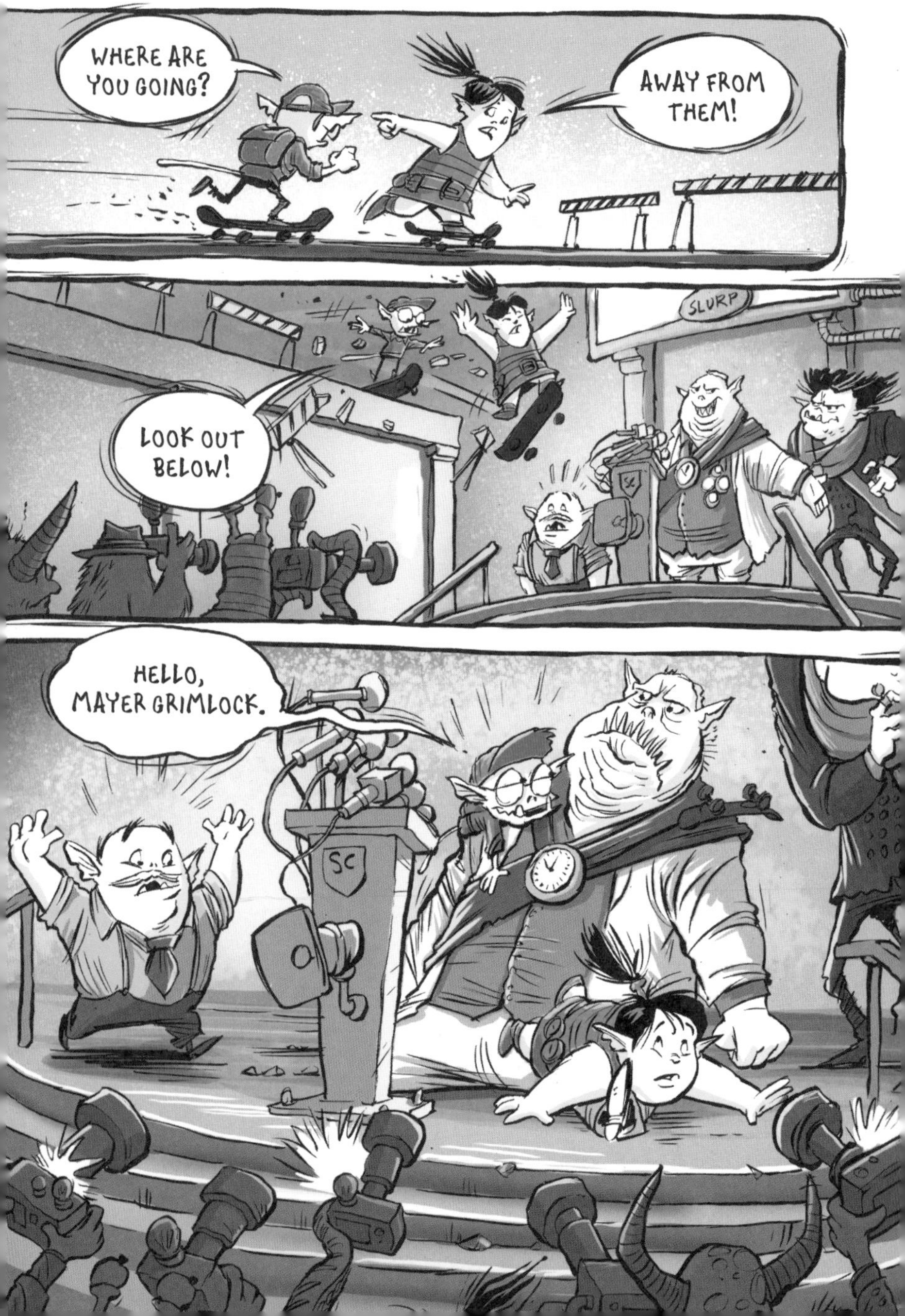
WHERE ARE YOU GOING?
AWAY FROM THEM!
SLURP
LOOK OUT BELOW!
HELLO, MAYER GRIMLOCK.

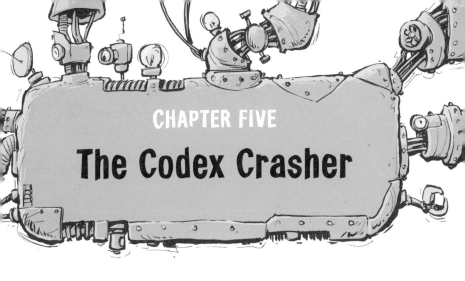

CHAPTER FIVE
The Codex Crasher

Everything was a mess of scrambling security guards, snapping cameras and screaming goblins.

Okay, that last one was me. But someone had me by the tail and was yanking really hard.

It was the mayor.

I had landed on his head, still riding my skateboard. Not a bad trick, but Mayor Grimlock didn't see it that way. In fact, at this particular moment he didn't see much of anything.

"Get off me, you filthy pest!" he snarled.

I scrambled off the mayor and fell to the ground. I landed beside Tank under the glare of many cameras.

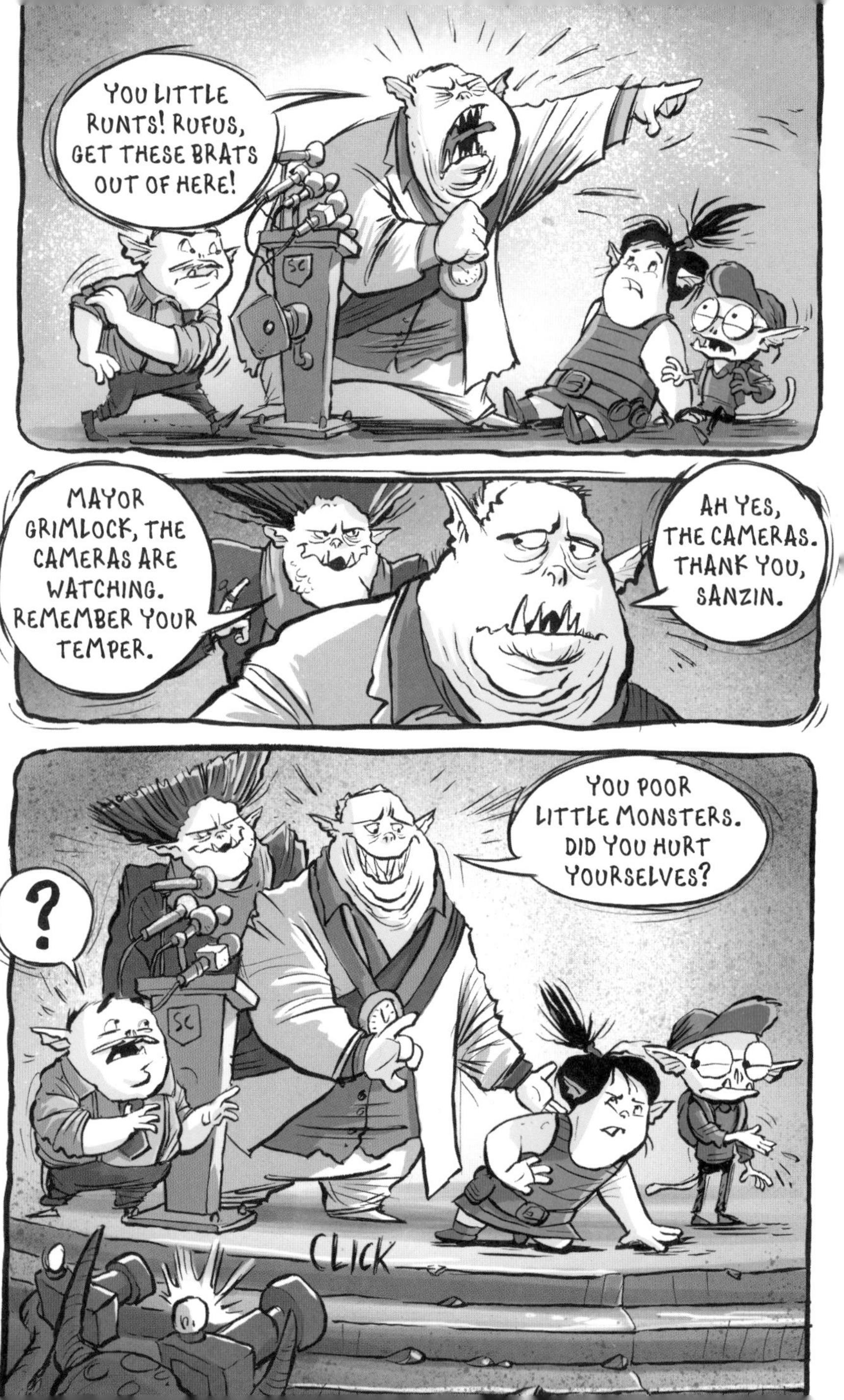
YOU LITTLE RUNTS! RUFUS, GET THESE BRATS OUT OF HERE!
SC
MAYOR GRIMLOCK, THE CAMERAS ARE WATCHING. REMEMBER YOUR TEMPER.
AH YES, THE CAMERAS. THANK YOU, SANZIN.
YOU POOR LITTLE MONSTERS. DID YOU HURT YOURSELVES?
?
SC
CLICK

The cameras went crazy, snapping photos of Mayor Grimlock helping Tank and me to our feet. Rufus, the mayor's goblin assistant, shuffled us off to one side.

Sanzin stepped in front of us and addressed the reporters.

"Amazing! Mayor Grimlock saves two darling monsters with his own body!" The troll's black hair was gelled to perfection, and his suit was pressed to match. Gem-encrusted rings covered his fingers, and around his neck hung a pendant holding a single purple jewel. Sanzin flashed a sparkling smile to the gathered reporters. "As president of SlurpCo Industries, I'm proud to say our mayor is a hero! Because of his selflessness, these two darling little monsters have been spared from harm."

I wasn't sure what planet big, tall and warty was on. It definitely wasn't the one where Tank and I squashed the mayor of Slick City. But if it was a planet where Tank and I didn't get in trouble for squashing the mayor, I was fine with it.

"Fizzy!" a voice cried out from the pack of reporters.

Rana Marlow, also known as Mom, pushed her way to the front of the crowd. She scooped me up in a big hug and checked me over for broken bones. "Are you okay?"

I wasn't surprised my mom was here. She is a reporter for the city's biggest newspaper. She's always following Mayor Grimlock to press conferences like this one.

"What are you two doing here?" she said once she'd decided nothing was broken.

"It's a long story, Mom," I said, wriggling free. Don't get me wrong. Mom's hugs are great. But the way Tank was giggling, I knew I'd be hearing about the whole "Fizzy" business for the next week.

"Tank!" Mom said, as if noticing her for the first time. "Are you all right?"

"I'm fine, Ms. Marlow," she said.

Beside us, Rufus adjusted the mayor's jacket and gave him a final check for broken bones. Mayor Grimlock pushed his assistant aside and glared at the three of us.

The smooth-talking troll ushered us away from the mayor.

"If mother-son time is over, Rana, we have a press conference to get started." Sanzin's words were colder than an ice dragon's sneeze.

"All right, Sanzin, don't pop a wart," Mom snapped.

Everything the tall troll wore was black. His expensive-looking business suit with its sharp-angled shoulders was dark like his hair and eyes. The only sign of color was the purple jewel in the pendant around his neck. Even in the dimming glowshroom light, the stone sparkled brightly. It was as if it had its own source of energy.

"You're not in charge, remember?" my mom said. She wasn't done with Sanzin. "Your precious mayor will get his chance to brag about his new stadium after I make sure he didn't hurt these innocent children."

Before the troll could respond, Mom dragged us back into the crowd of reporters.

"What are you two doing here?" she said when we got to the back of the pack.

We quickly told Mom about Rizzo, the battle bots and the weird face on the billboard.

"That does sound strange," she said when we were finished. "Lucky for you, my editor sent me down here to cover this press conference."

"I thought you weren't covering fluff stories about the mayor anymore, Mom."

Mom's eyes flashed the way they do when she's on to a big story.

"We got a tip from a mysterious source that this press conference could get interesting," she said.

My mom has been a reporter for as long as I can remember. Like me, she has a tail for mysteries. She turns her mysteries into stories for her editors at the *Rockfall Times*.

"What's all this about anyway?" Tank said.

"Mayor Grimlock wants to show off his shiny new stadium," said a goblin holding an extend-o-camera. Mom shared a knowing smile with the reporter.

"Any chance for him to look good for the cameras, right, Lex?" she said.

Lex fiddled with the focus controls on his camera. "It's hard to make an ogre that ugly look good."

That got a chuckle out of the other reporters around us. Trolls, goblins and ogres from the big TV companies stood with their cameras, waiting for the mayor's big announcement. There must have been reporters from all the major news organizations in Rockfall Mountain here. There were even a few bug-eyed critters from the smaller newspapers based deep in the mountain near the Dark Depths.

"Grimlock has been bragging about this stadium for months," Mom said. "Many people in Slick City didn't want it built. They said it would cost too much money."

"But he built it anyway?" Tank asked.

"Yep," Mom said. "He paved over a park, knocked down a few buildings and moved some monsters out of their homes just to build it right here."

"Why not build it somewhere else?"

"SlurpCo Industries," Lex said. "And their fearless leader, Sanzin Balazar."

Lex pointed his camera at the troll in black and snapped a picture.

"That's the company that owns all those slick-drilling rigs in the harbor," Mom said.

"It also owns the construction company that built the stadium and the security company that patrols it at night," Lex said. "The company paid a lot of money to get the stadium built. They insisted it be built right on this spot."

"So that's why it's called Slurp Stadium," I said.

The screech of a microphone stopped the chatter of the other reporters. All eyes went to the podium at the top of the steps leading to the stadium.

Mayor Grimlock stood at the podium. He flashed that election-winning smile we had all seen on screens across the city. From this close, I could see just how sharp the mayor's fangs really were.

"Greetings! And many thanks for coming out this afternoon," he crooned. Although an ugly ogre, Mayor Grimlock spoke with words as sweet as nectar on a stack of hollowberry cakes. Hearing him talk, it was no surprise he had been elected mayor three times in a row. He knew how to pour on the charm. "Today is a day to be remembered! Slurp Stadium is nearly complete. Next week, during the grand opening, another jewel will be added to beautiful Slick City!"

"Beautiful Slick City? Mayor Grimlock needs to get out more," Lex said under his breath.

Slick City is built on one thing—slick. Mucky, black liquid sucked from rocks and used to run everything from our cars to our phones. It is messy and stinky, but it has made a few monsters very rich. Slick City has been called many things, but only a monster who couldn't see, smell or taste would call it *beautiful*. Or a mayor who will say anything to get reelected.

"Thanks to our partners at SlurpCo Industries," Mayor Grimlock continued, "this stadium will be a beacon of sport and entertainment. To mark the grand opening, the Slick City Battle Bot Cup will be held here. Just watch the screen above me and feast your eyes on what Slurp Stadium has to offer!"

The mayor swept his fat arm up to the jumbo screen hanging over the stadium's main entrance.

The screen jumped to life in a whirl of flashing colors. The SlurpCo Industries logo swirled onto the screen. The logo faded away, replaced by the wide, grinning face of Mayor Grimlock. He stood in the middle of the stadium playing field where the battle-bot arena had been set up.

"Hello from the heart of Slurp Stadium!" his voice crooned from the screen's speakers.

The live Mayor Grimlock looked up at his likeness on-screen. He grinned like a rust hound after an all-you-can eat junkyard buffet.

The mayor on the screen led the viewers on a tour of the brand-new stadium. He piloted a shiny new battle bot around the battle-bot field. Then he was at the concession stand, chomping on a spicy lizard dog smothered in glowshroom mustard.

My stomach rumbled. I thought about the plate of choco-slug cookies waiting for me at home.

Mayor Grimlock was in mid-bite when the screen went black. A second later, it buzzed back to life with a new image.

GREETINGS, SLICK CITY! THIS IS THE CODEX WITH A MESSAGE FOR MAYOR GRIMLOCK AND HIS SLURPCO FRIENDS.

SLURP

The press went into snapshot overload. Mayor Grimlock looked like he was ready to explode. He swatted at Rufus, who was doing his best to regain control of the stadium's giant screen.

"Finally this press conference gets interesting," Lex said as he captured the chaos with his camera.

"Looks like your tip was right, Mom," I said.

Mom wrote in her notebook as fast as her pen would move. She had her story for the next day's paper.

This wasn't the first time the Codex had messed with the mayor. The mysterious Codex had appeared shortly after construction on Slurp Stadium began. He'd demanded that the mayor close down the stadium. Grimlock refused, and the Codex had been making life miserable for the mayor and all Slurp Stadium supporters ever since.

The Codex was a master computer hacker. In the past few months, he had hijacked all the computers at city hall, where the mayor works, and locked everyone out of their phones and vizpaper tablets. Grimlock had to shut down city hall for two days until they got control of their computers again. And about a month ago, the Codex took over all the TV channels in the city. Everyone's screens went blank for over three hours and were replaced with a sign that read *Close Slurp Stadium.*

The Codex had never been caught. And no one knew who he was. Or even if it was a he. It could be a she. No one knew who the Codex was, but everyone in Slick City had felt his—or her—power.

Rufus scrambled around the podium, frantically pulling out power cords and wires. Nothing he did turned off the large screen or made the smiling face of the Codex disappear. Mayor Grimlock chased his assistant around the controls, barking at the poor goblin to pull the cords out faster. In the chaos on the stage, only Sanzin Balazar looked in control. The troll stood perfectly still and glared at the image of the Codex as if he could melt the jumbo screen with his eyes.

Lex adjusted the settings on his camera, chuckling at the images he was catching. My mom kept grinning and scribbling the story into her notepad.

They might have been feeling good about the mayor's disaster, but I felt like I'd eaten a boulder sandwich. Tank couldn't take her eyes off the screen either.

"You recognize that face?" I asked.

She nodded. "It's the guy Rizzo was talking to earlier."

"Rizzo Rawlins is dealing with the Codex."

Our little task of catching a cheat had just gotten as big as the stadium in front of us.

CHAPTER SIX

Smoothie Talking

The Bouncing Bugbear was packed.

Young monsters from all over Slick City came to the diner to meet friends, complain about school and enjoy one of Rita the bugbear's delicious fungi-fruit smoothies.

Today, Rita wasn't actually bouncing. She was rolling, and so were her waiters. The fat rollers on their feet let them zip from table to table, bringing burgers, shakes and delicious cakes to hungry trolls, ogres, goblins and elves.

"Howdy, little detectives," Rita called when she spotted Tank and me coming through the front door. She rolled right up to us, balancing a large tray of basilisk burgers in one hand. "There's a booth at the back with your name on it."

"Thanks, R!" Tank said.

"Anytime, T!" Rita rolled away to deliver the burgers to a table of hungry ogres.

Tank and I found the booth and got to work. We had been stuck in school all day with no time to talk about the previous day's press conference or Rizzo's meeting with the mysterious Codex.

Tank spread a thin sheet of vizpaper on the table.

"I salvaged the hard drive from my spybot last night," she said. She tapped the paper and it lit up, filling our booth with a soft green glow.

"The bot Rizzo stepped on?" I said. "I thought it was lost forever in that parking lot."

"Thankfully, he didn't damage its homing circuits," she said with a smile. "The little bot flew back home. It barely made it. Dreena and Draana found it stuck on a glowshroom outside our front door."

"Hooray for little sisters," I said.

Tank smiled and tapped the paper again. A series of images appeared on the thin sheet of glass.

"I couldn't get the video out of the hard drive, thanks to Rizzo's boot. But I salvaged these screen shots."

The photos showed Rizzo and the Gutro brothers talking to the Codex. The mysterious stranger's mask loomed over them from the billboard.

"I still can't believe that Rizzo is working with the Codex," I said.

Rita rolled up to our table. She dropped two large bugberry smoothies in front of us.

"Here's your usual, detectives," she said with a smile. "I knew you would be too busy solving your latest mystery to actually remember to order!"

"Thanks, Rita!" I said. Rita rolled away with a wave over her shoulder.

I slurped up some bugberry smoothie. The icy drink sent a chill along my scales and froze my brain. I always think better after a good bugberry brain freeze.

Tank sipped on her frosty drink as she swiped through the images on the vizpaper. She stopped on a close-up of Rizzo talking to the Codex on the billboard. "How does a kid in the fourth grade get in contact with a mysterious hacker tormenting the mayor?" she said.

"Ratso Rawlins is Rizzo's dad. That old kobold knows all the bigwigs in the city," I said after my brain had thawed. "Maybe Rizzo met the Codex at one of the Rawlins family's night-howl parties?"

"Maybe, but Ratso Rawlins is also one of Mayor Grimlock's biggest supporters," Tank said. "The Codex doesn't like the mayor or Slurp Stadium. I don't think Ratso Rawlins would be happy to hear his son is friends with the mayor's enemies."

Tank and I finished our smoothies in silence. My mind chased questions as I fished out the last goopy drops of my smoothie.

"Who is the Codex?" I said finally. "Why does he want Slurp Stadium closed?"

A shadow fell across our table.

"Because that stadium is an ugly pile of concrete?"

Aleetha used to be in our class at Gravelmuck Elementary. Now she goes to the wizard's school in the Shadow Tower. All lava elves apply to the Shadow Tower when they're our age. Not many get accepted, but Aleetha did. She's been studying magic ever since and is destined to be a great wizard someday. She's already a pretty good detective. Her magical knowledge has helped Tank and me in the past. Now that the Codex was part of this mystery, we needed all the help we could get.

Aleetha slid into the booth beside Tank.

"What's Rizzo up to now?"

After yesterday's press conference, Tank sent a message to Aleetha telling her about Rizzo and the Codex. We had so many questions, we needed Aleetha's brainpower to get some answers. It turned out she had just as many questions as we did.

"Why is Rizzo talking to weird faces on billboards?" Aleetha thumbed through the photos on Tank's vizpaper.

"That's the Codex," I said. "The guy who took over the press conference."

"Interesting," Aleetha said. "His face looks familiar."

"It looks like a mask to me," Tank said. "It's drawn with computer graphics, like a video-game character."

"He's hiding his real identity," I said.

"Or *her* real identity." Aleetha zoomed in on the photo of the Codex's face. "I've seen that mask somewhere before."

"He was all over the TV in last night's news," Tank said.

Aleetha shook her head. "TVs don't work inside the Shadow Tower. I've seen this somewhere else."

"Whoever he or she is, the Codex doesn't want Slurp Stadium to open," I said.

"He's not alone," Aleetha said. "A lot of people are upset about that stadium. It's ugly, for one thing. It also cost a lot of money to build, and Mayor Grimlock kicked a lot of people out of their homes just to make space for it."

"So the Codex could be just about anyone in Slick City?" Tank said.

"Anyone with the technical skills to take over the mayor's computers," Aleetha said. "How did you end up on the trail of the Codex?"

"Technically we're not," I said. "We're trying to prove Rizzo is cheating in the battle-bot fights."

"How's he doing that?"

"With this," Tank said. She tapped the vizpaper and brought up a photo of Rizzo fishing the Codex's computer equipment out of a garbage can.

"Whatever that is," I said.

Aleetha scrunched up her nose at the sight of the equipment in the photo.

"Don't look at me to help you," she said. "That's got technology written all over it. You need to talk to a troll."

"My troll is stumped," I said.

That got me a swat across the head from Tank, but it was worth it.

"I am not stumped," Tank said. "It's a processor unit. A high-quality one. Just the thing to make his battle bot move fast. We need to prove that Rizzo installed it in his battle bot."

"He's already busted me for snooping twice," I said. "I'm not eager to try for a third time."

Aleetha scrolled through the other photos on the vizpaper. "I could ask our battle-bot team. They might know something."

"The Shadow Tower has a battle-bot team?" Tank said. "I thought wizards couldn't use technology."

"We can't, but we can use our magic. We enchant the metal and make it do what we want."

"Not fair!" Tank said.

"Relax," Aleetha said. "We are only wizards-in-training. Our enchantments are limited. Trust me. It's all fair."

"Makes sense," I said. "The other battle-bot competitors have to build their own bots and write their own code."

"Unless your name is Rizzo Rawlins," Tank grumbled.

The TV at the front of the diner suddenly became louder. Rita had the TV remote in her large paw and was turning up the volume on the screen hanging on the wall.

On the screen, a young news reporter was talking so fast that she struggled to catch her breath.

"It all started downtown about an hour ago," the reporter said. She waved her arms around like she was doing some new dance. "That's when monsters across Slick City lost control of their technology. All thanks to this mysterious figure."

A familiar purple face appeared on the news report.

"The Codex!" Tank and I said together.

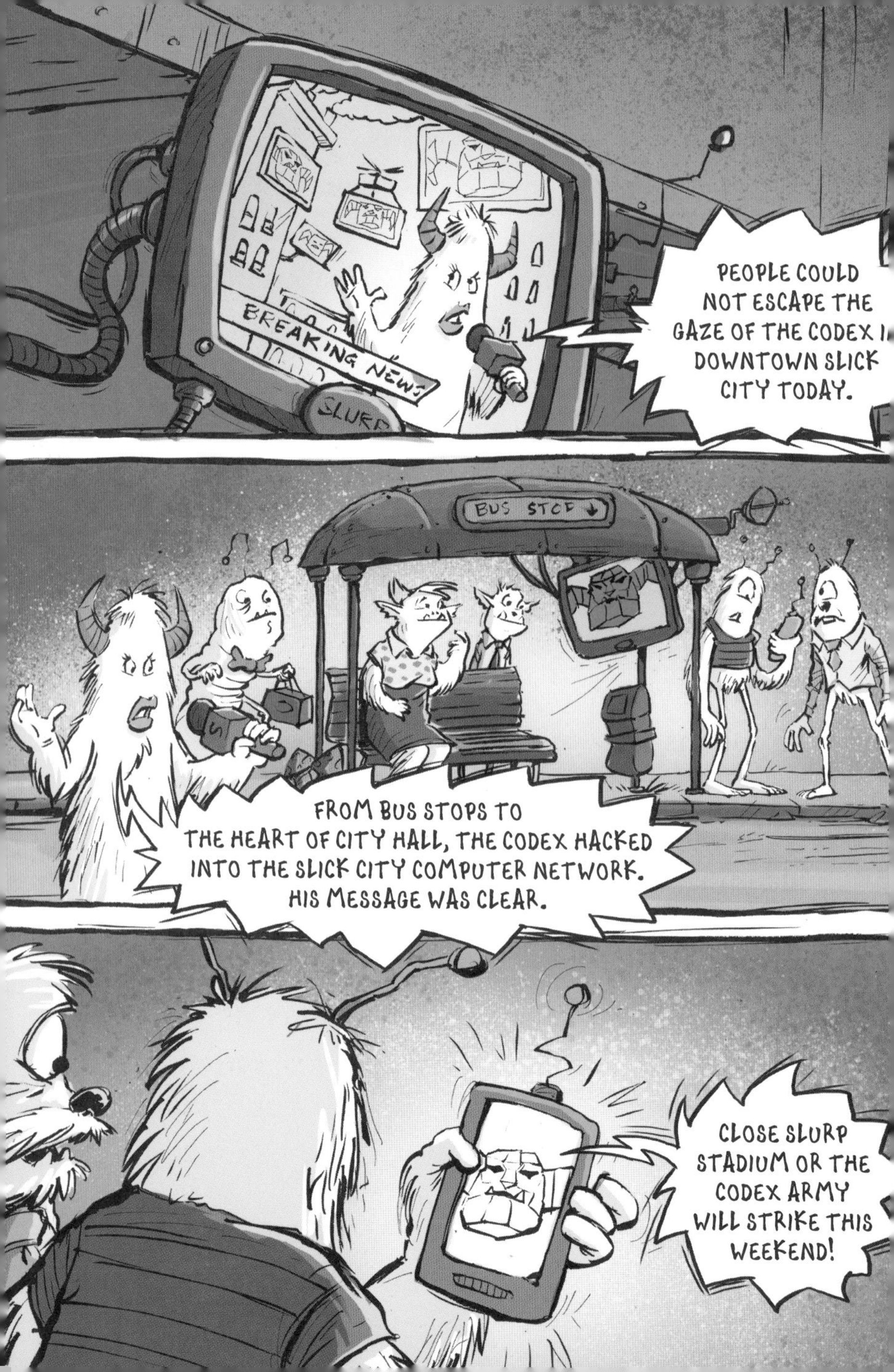
BREAKING NEWS
PEOPLE COULD NOT ESCAPE THE GAZE OF THE CODEX I
DOWNTOWN SLICK CITY TODAY.
BUS STOP
FROM BUS STOPS TO THE HEART OF CITY HALL, THE CODEX HACKED INTO THE SLICK CITY COMPUTER NETWORK. HIS MESSAGE WAS CLEAR.
CLOSE SLURP STADIUM OR THE CODEX ARMY WILL STRIKE THIS WEEKEND!

The TV news cut to the weather report. Rita turned down the volume. The bugbear rolled over to a table of goblins and joined them in talking about the strange news story.

"Did you hear that?" Aleetha said. "The Codex is planning to strike during the Slurp Stadium grand opening this weekend."

"The Battle Bot Cup is part of the grand opening," Tank said. "Do you think they're connected?"

"Could be," Aleetha said. Her fiery red eyes glowed with curiosity. Once she got hold of an unsolved problem, Aleetha couldn't let go. "Who or what is the Codex Army?"

I scrolled through the photos again until I found the one I wanted.

"I think we already know one of the Codex's soldiers," I said.

The image of Rizzo talking to the Codex stared up at all of us.

No one spoke, but I knew we were all thinking the same thing.

Rizzo was part of the Codex Army.

CHAPTER SEVEN

Slippery Kobolds

The next morning, Tank met me at the school gates.

"You got here just in time," she said.

"In time for what?"

"Hopefully, to hear Rizzo confess."

A high-pitched yelp came from near the bike racks. We hurried around the side of the school.

Rizzo Rawlins faced off against the whole Troll Patrol squad. There was no sign of the Gutro twins. Daztan had him by his shirt collar. The kobold's furry feet dangled off the ground.

Tank turned to me. "This wasn't my idea, Fizz. I told them hurting Rizzo wouldn't help our case. But there was no stopping them."

Rizzo snarled, snapped and growled, but he could not break free from the troll's tight grip.

"Put me down, you big wart sack!" he yelped.

"Not so tough without your goons, are you, Rizzo?" Daztan said.

"They'll be here soon, Daztan," Rizzo snapped.

Ryla moved in close to the dangling kobold.

"Then we have time to ask you a few questions." She held up a piece of vizpaper and poked Rizzo in the belly with her long finger. "Care to explain what you're doing in these photos?"

"This is all my fault," Tank said under her breath to me. She tugged with worry at the pockets of her tool belt. "I showed the Troll Patrol my photos of Rizzo meeting the Codex."

"And they decided to take matters into their own claws," I said.

"Daztan and the others are still angry about losing to Rizzo," Tank said.

"I can see that." I stepped closer to Daztan. "Put the kobold down, Daz. We can get answers from him without risking a trip to Weaver's office."

"He'll just run." Daztan grunted. "Kobolds always run."

"He'll stay and answer some questions." I turned to Rizzo. "Won't you?"

Rizzo's beady eyes jumped to each of us, sizing up his chances of actually running free from three trolls much older than him. Even a kobold like Rizzo could do that math.

"I'll stay," he muttered. "But keep your claws off my fur!"

Daztan let go of Rizzo. The kobold dropped to the ground but didn't run. For now. We didn't have much time. The Gutro twins would arrive at school soon and tip the scales back in Rizzo's favor.

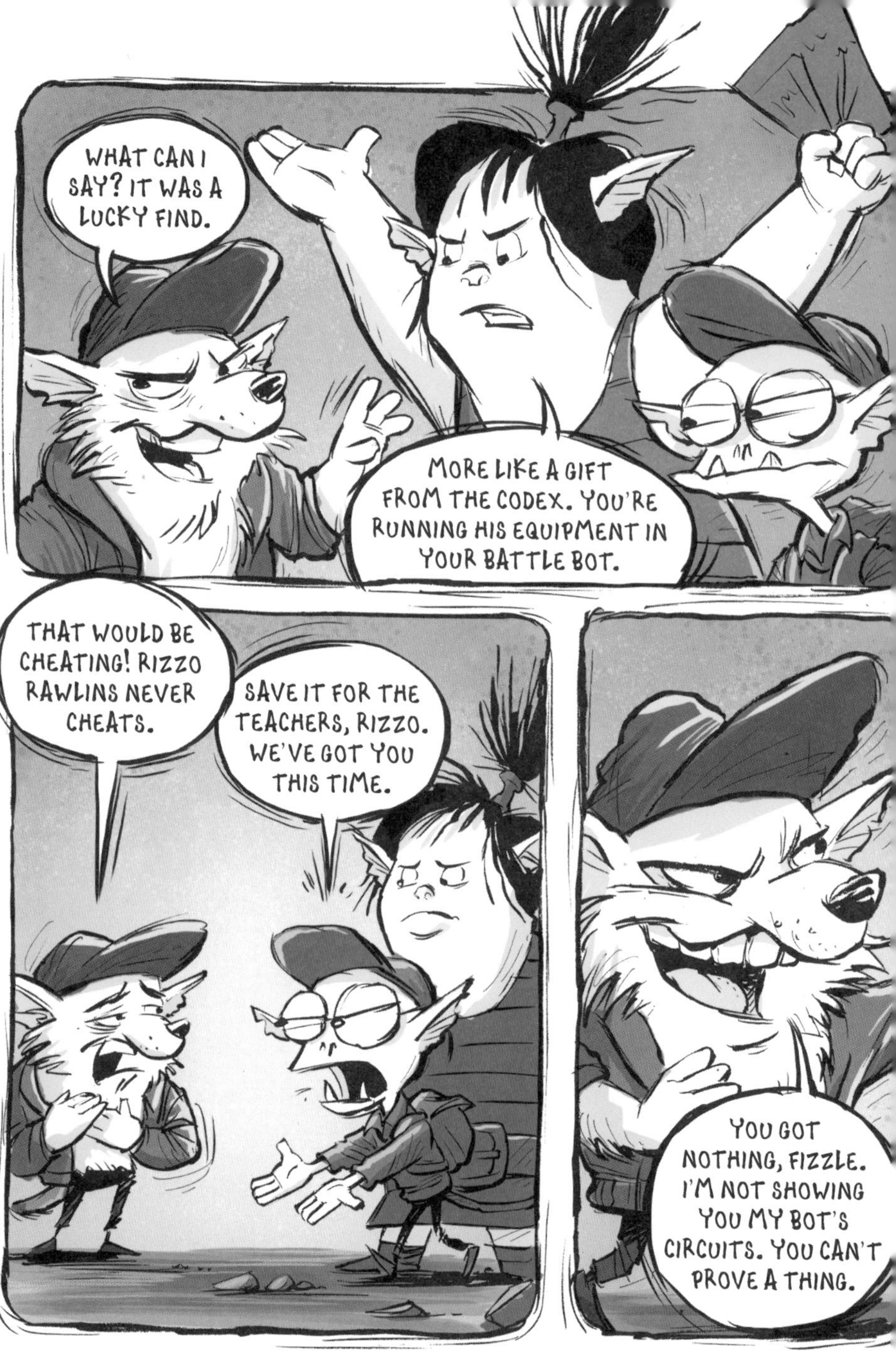
WHAT CAN I SAY? IT WAS A LUCKY FIND.
MORE LIKE A GIFT FROM THE CODEX. YOU'RE RUNNING HIS EQUIPMENT IN YOUR BATTLE BOT.
THAT WOULD BE CHEATING! RIZZO RAWLINS NEVER CHEATS.
SAVE IT FOR THE TEACHERS, RIZZO. WE'VE GOT YOU THIS TIME.
YOU GOT NOTHING, FIZZLE. I'M NOT SHOWING YOU MY BOT'S CIRCUITS. YOU CAN'T PROVE A THING.

The smelly kobold had a point. The only way we could prove Rizzo was using the Codex's battle-bot equipment was to actually see it installed in his battle bot. Like Rizzo said, that wasn't happening. Only Principal Weaver could force Rizzo to show us what was under his bot's armored casing. That old web crawler thought Rizzo was a model student, so that wasn't happening either.

The school bell rang. Monsters from all over the schoolyard shuffled into the school, ready to get the day started.

"I believe we are done here," Rizzo said. He licked his snout with satisfaction. "I don't have time to be bothered with this nonsense again. I have the city-wide battle-bot finals to prepare for. Out of my way!"

The kobold pushed through us and headed into the school. His laughter rang in my ears long after he had gone inside.

Disappointment was written on the faces of the Troll Patrol. Rizzo Rawlins just couldn't lose. He had won the school battle-bot finals and proved our only piece of evidence useless.

The day had just begun and already I was wishing I could crawl back into bed.

By the end of the school day, my mood had not improved. Rizzo was still going to get away with cheating, and I had a fresh pile of homework to deal with.

I planned to head home and drown my sorrows with a stack of choco-slug cookies and some video games.

Tank caught up with me at my locker. She was out of breath.

"Grab your stuff, Fizz. We don't have much time."

"Time?" I said. "Time for what?"

Tank looked at me. "Did you turn off your phone again?"

I had. I'm not anti-tech or anything—I just don't like the idea of a phone always tracking where I'm going. Of course, when I turn it off I miss getting messages. Like the one Aleetha had sent Tank and me a few minutes ago.

Our friend's message appeared on my phone's screen when I turned it on. It was short and to the point:

Twenty minutes later, we hopped off our boards in unfamiliar territory.

"The Mage District," I said. "I've never actually been here before."

"Me neither," Tank said. She curled her nose. "It smells of magic."

The Mage District was a warren of twisty streets and narrow alleys lined with booksellers, scroll merchants and traders of magical knowledge of all kinds. Behind us, Slurp Stadium dominated the skyline. Much closer and much taller, the Shadow Tower loomed.

"I isolated the trace-back data from Aleetha's message." Tank walked in a slow circle with her eyes on her phone. She stopped suddenly and looked up. "The call came from inside that building."

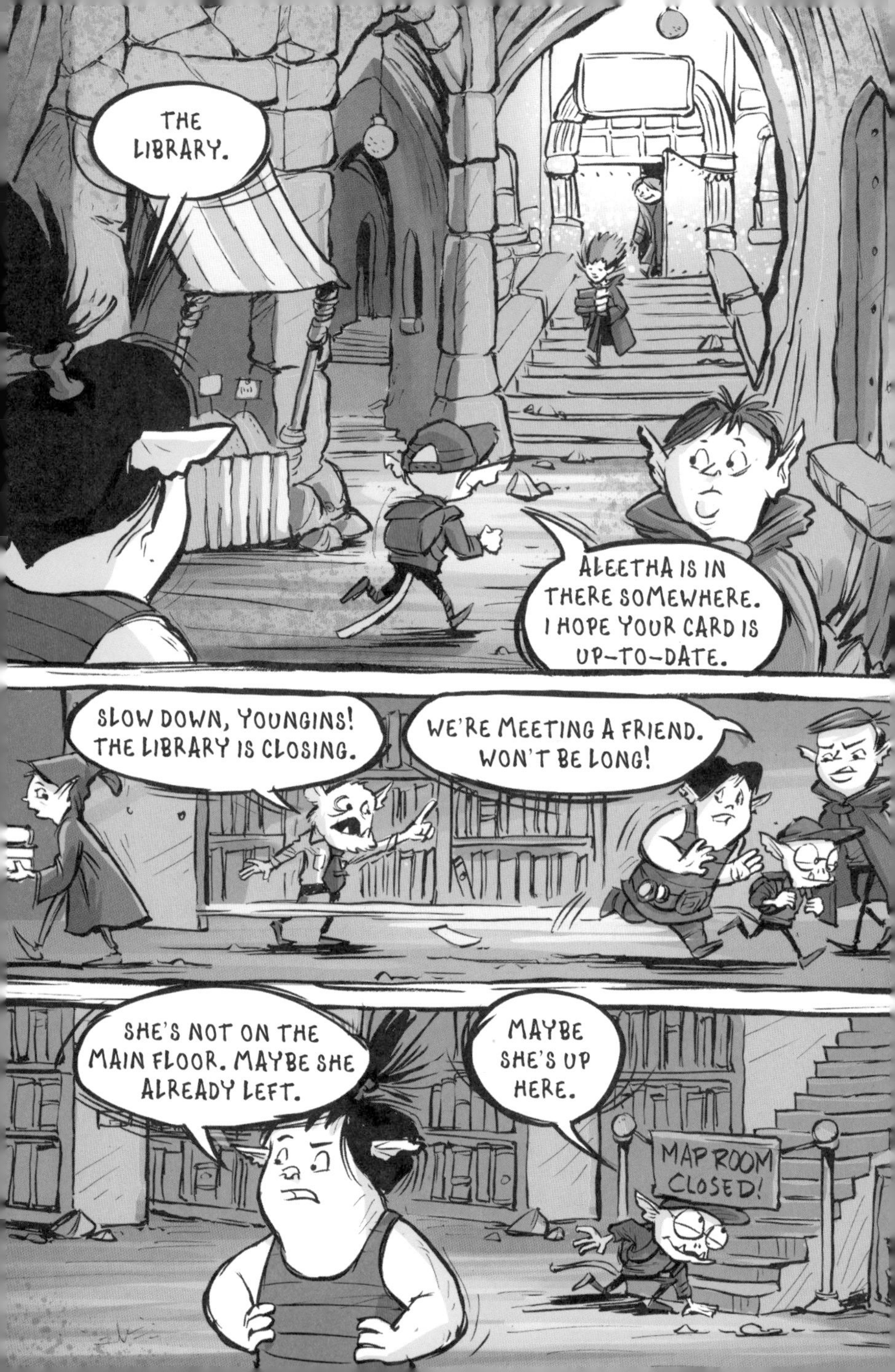
THE LIBRARY.
ALEETHA IS IN THERE SOMEWHERE. I HOPE YOUR CARD IS UP-TO-DATE.
SLOW DOWN, YOUNGINS! THE LIBRARY IS CLOSING.
WE'RE MEETING A FRIEND. WON'T BE LONG!
SHE'S NOT ON THE MAIN FLOOR. MAYBE SHE ALREADY LEFT.
MAYBE SHE'S UP HERE.
MAP ROOM CLOSED!

The upper floor of the library was completely dark. Thankfully, goblins and dark go well together. I could make out the rows of shelves stretching into the shadows. Each shelf was packed with books, scrolls and bound parchment.

Tank's eyes never left her phone screen. She led the way through the dark.

"Aleetha isn't answering my calls," she said as she went. "But we're getting close to her phone's signal source."

She hurried between two rows of shelves packed with dusty scrolls, then stopped.

On the ground at Tank's feet, something small sparkled with magic.

"Aleetha's phone," I said.

"But no Aleetha," Tank said.

A terrifying roar split the darkness.

The roar was quickly followed by a scream.

Tank's eyes locked with mine.

"Aleetha!"

CHAPTER EIGHT

Dangerous Books

Running toward screams in the dark is never a good idea. But when the screams belong to your friend, good ideas get tossed out the window.

Tank rushed between the rows of shelves with me close behind.

The screams led us to a round, shelf-lined room with a few dusty chairs and tables. It must have been some sort of study hall. Now it looked like a battle arena. Aleetha stood on top of a table in the middle of the room, facing an enemy unlike anything I had ever seen.

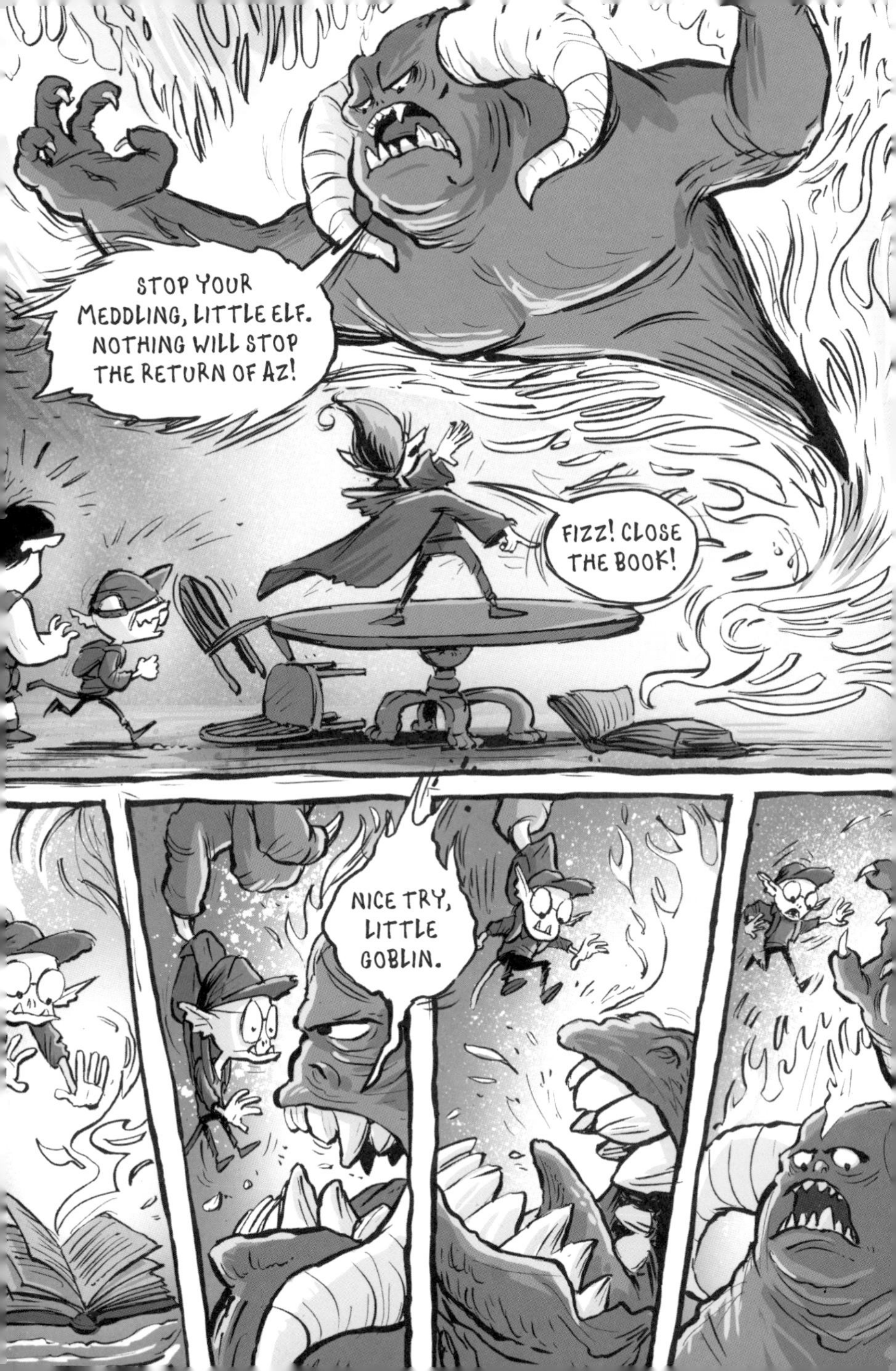
STOP YOUR MEDDLING, LITTLE ELF. NOTHING WILL STOP THE RETURN OF AZ!
FIZZ! CLOSE THE BOOK!
NICE TRY, LITTLE GOBLIN.

The only sound in the room was our breathing.
Aleetha eyed the thick book under Tank's feet as if it
might jump to life and attack again.

"That book is trapped," she said. "I came up here
looking for old maps of Slick City. That book was
waiting for me."

"Waiting for you?" I asked. "How can a book be
waiting for you?"

"Never underestimate a book, Fizz," Aleetha said. Her fiery red eyes pierced the gloom of the study hall. She approached the book slowly. "Even the most mundane tome has the ability to touch the reader."

"That book definitely touched me!" I rubbed my neck where the scaly demon had grabbed me.

Aleetha examined the book, careful not to get too close.

"This book is enchanted with a guardian spell. That's what attacked us." She glanced up at the shelves around us. "This is the map room. Only maps and old sea charts should be up here."

"But this book was here too?" Tank said, her foot still firmly pressing the book closed.

"Right beside the map I was looking for," Aleetha said. "I took the map from the shelf and the book jumped off too."

"Jumped?" I said. "Books can't jump."

"Tell that to whatever is inside these pages," Aleetha said. She reached deep into the folds of her mage's robes and pulled out something small and metallic. "This book doesn't belong here. Someone put it next to the old maps of Slick City."

"Someone who didn't want you to see the maps," I said.

"Exactly." Aleetha gingerly fiddled with the side of the book. There was a solid snapping noise, like metal connecting with metal. When the lava elf stepped away from the book, a small but sturdy padlock held the covers of the book firmly closed.

"You can step away, Tank," she said. "I think we have silenced the book's guardian for now."

"For now?" Tank said. She slowly stepped off the thick book. She eyed the padlock suspiciously.

"It's just a practice lock for enchantments and stuff," Aleetha said. "It's designed to keep greedy roommates out of my food cupboard."

"And now it's the only thing keeping us safe from a magical guardian with a taste for goblins?" I moved behind a large table, just to be on the safe side.

"If this book was up here waiting for you, then that means..."

"Someone knew I was coming," Aleetha finished.

"But who?" Tank said.

Aleetha's eyes fell to the cover of the book on the floor.

A familiar face stared back at us.

"The Codex!"

On the cover of the book that had nearly eaten the three of us, the calm purple face of the Codex stared out at us.

"*Azaralath: Keeper of the Fire,*" I said, reading the cover of the book.

"Who is Azaralath?" Tank said. "And why does he look like the Codex?"

"Azaralath, also known as Az," Aleetha said. "I knew I had seen the Codex's face before. We studied all the old demons in history class. It's hard to forget a face like Az's."

"Demons?" I said. The scales on my neck stood on end. "Az is a demon?"

Tank took another step away from the padlocked book. "I thought demons had all been banished back to their home worlds."

"I did too," Aleetha said.

"Codex the hacker is really a demon?" Tank said.

"No," Aleetha said. "Az the demon was banished centuries ago. The Codex is probably just some monster using the demon's face to scare us."

"It's working," Tank muttered. She didn't take her eyes off the book.

So the mystery hacker we'd seen on the jumbo screen at Slurp Stadium was using the face of a banished demon to scare Slick City. Tank was right. It was working. No matter where I went in that dark room, the eyes staring from the cover of the book followed me.

"Can we go now?" Tank said. "We saved you from big, bad and bookish."

Aleetha didn't answer. She took a dusty scroll from the shelf and spread it across a table. She stood on a chair and leaned over the scroll, studying it closely.

"Interesting," she said. She was too deep in her own ideas to hear Tank. "Look at this."

The scroll nearly reached both sides of the table. Faded lines ran across the parchment.

"A map," I said.

"An old goblin map, to be precise," Aleetha said. "It's a map of Slick City before it became Slick City."

"How's that?" Tank tilted to one side like she was looking for a secret message hidden in the map.

"It was created by the goblins before the ogres came and settled Slick City," Aleetha said.

"You mean before the ogres *took* the land from the goblins," I said. "My goblin ancestors were here fishing in Fang Harbor long before the ogres showed up. They kicked us off our land so they could drill for slick."

Tank nodded. "And they've been pulling the goopy stuff out of the rocks ever since."

"All very true," Aleetha said. "And it means this map is old. Very old."

"Why are we looking at something old?" Tank said.

"Because I have a feeling old secrets are causing new troubles today," Aleetha said.

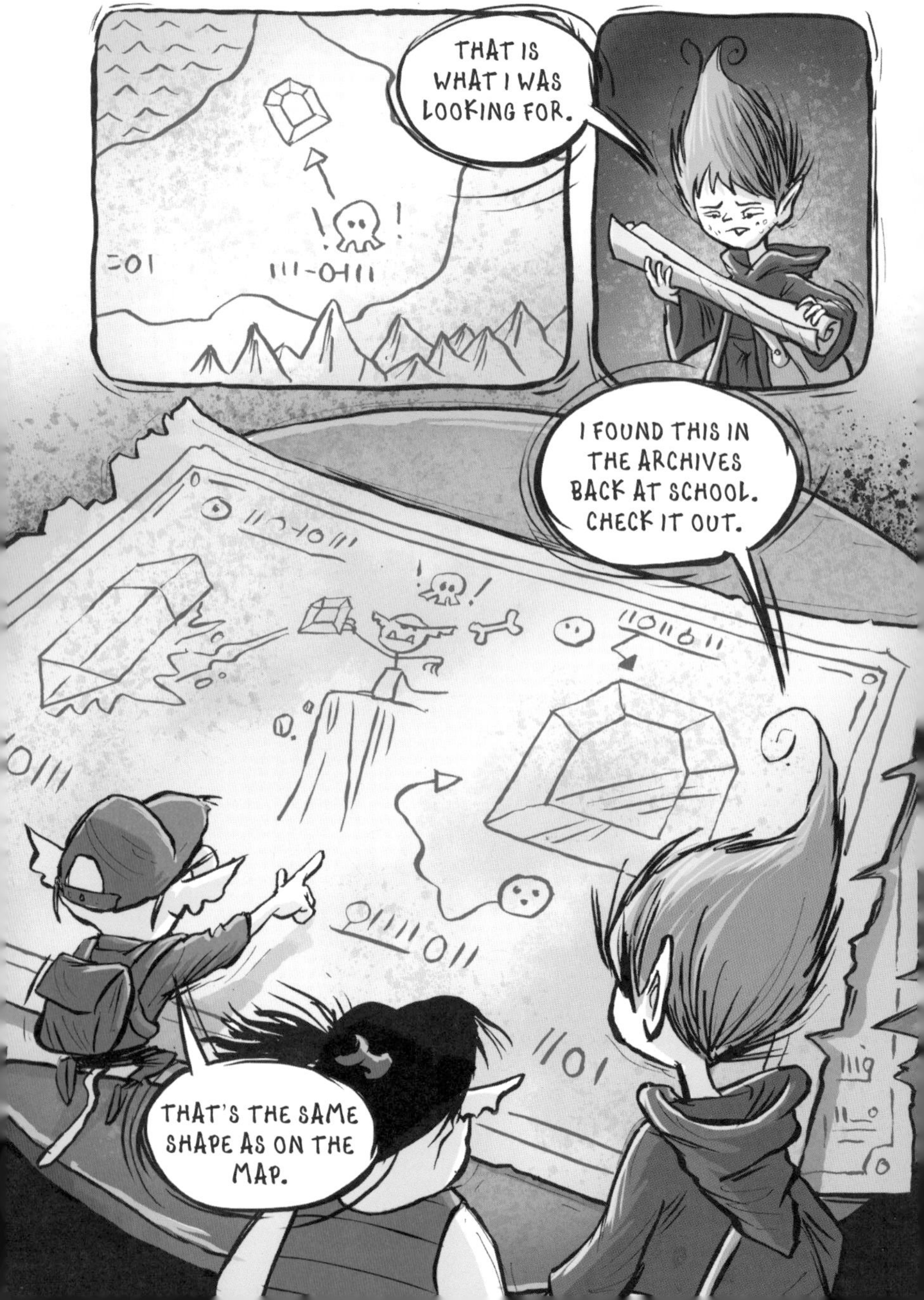
THAT IS WHAT I WAS LOOKING FOR.
I FOUND THIS IN THE ARCHIVES BACK AT SCHOOL. CHECK IT OUT.
THAT'S THE SAME SHAPE AS ON THE MAP.

CHAPTER NINE

Rooftop Bot Run

Aleetha moved her parchment next to the map. The large shape on it was a perfect match to the one on the map. She drummed her elf fingers on the paper.

"These numbers under the shape are map coordinates," she said. "I looked them up on a current map of Slick City. They match the spot where the buildings were torn down to build the stadium."

"So you came here to see if they matched anything on the older maps," Tank said.

"Exactly," Aleetha said. "I made a copy. The original page is still in the Shadow Tower library. Now that I see the same shape on the map, I think they're connected. But I can't read the writing. It's written in an old goblin language."

Tank and Aleetha both turned to me.

"I can't help you," I said. "I can barely read modern goblin writing!"

I took a closer look at the paper with the little stick monster. The letters definitely didn't make any sense. But I could tell the monster was doing something to the big shape with the little shape in his hands.

"It looks like instructions," I said. "Like it's trying to tell you how to do something with the shapes."

Aleetha nodded. "Whatever it says, this spot was special for your ancestors, Fizz."

Books crashed to the floor in the shadows on the edge of the map room.

We froze, our questions silenced. My scales stood on end.

"We are being watched." Aleetha waved her hand and vanished in a cloud of purple sparks, like she was never there.

Now Tank and I were alone in the gloom.

"Where did she go?" I said. "I hate when she does that."

Tank ignored me and worked at one of the pockets of her tool belt.

"Don't get your tail in a knot, Fizz. I'm still here." Aleetha's voice came from nowhere and everywhere. "I'm just invisible, but it won't last long."

Heavy footsteps thumped the library's old stone floor. Whatever was out there was moving away from us, but that didn't do much to smooth my scales.

The dusty air of the map room wafted around me. It took me a moment to realize that Aleetha was pushing her way past me. Her voice came from the shadows in a whisper.

"We must follow those footsteps!"

"*Follow* the footsteps?" I exclaimed. "How about we *hide* from the footsteps?"

But it was no use. Tank was already charging into the shadows. She fumbled with her belt pockets as she ran.

Now I was alone with the goblin-eating, book-smashing whatever-was-out-there.

I raced after Tank as fast as my claws could take me.

I caught sight of her at the far end of a row of shelves. She had one foot through a small window leading outside.

"Hurry, Fizz!" she called when she saw me. "It's getting away!"

I hopped through the window in time to see Tank scramble up the fire escape and onto the roof of the library.

By the time I pulled myself onto the roof, she had yanked a pair of metallic spring contraptions from her belt and strapped them to her feet.

"Get on my back," she said. "Aleetha's already way ahead of us."

I threw my arms around Tank's neck.

"How did Aleetha get so far ahead?"

"She's wearing a pair of my springers."

"What are springers?"

"Hold on. You're about to find out."

OPEN YOUR EYES, FIZZ! WATCH FOR WHATEVER IT IS WE'RE CHASING!

DO I HAVE TO?

BOING

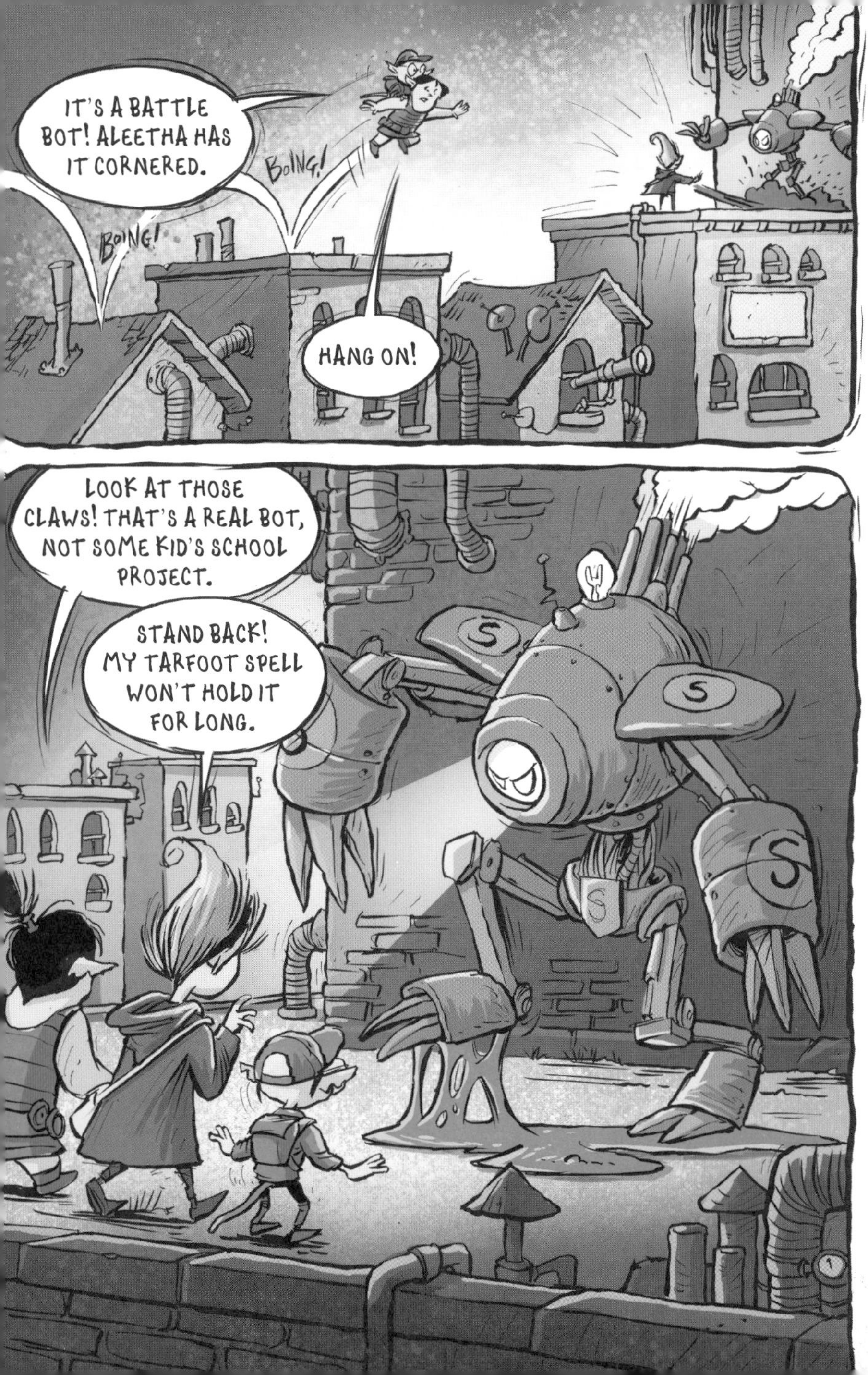
IT'S A BATTLE BOT! ALEETHA HAS IT CORNERED.
BOING!
BOING!
HANG ON!
LOOK AT THOSE CLAWS! THAT'S A REAL BOT, NOT SOME KID'S SCHOOL PROJECT.
STAND BACK! MY TARFOOT SPELL WON'T HOLD IT FOR LONG.

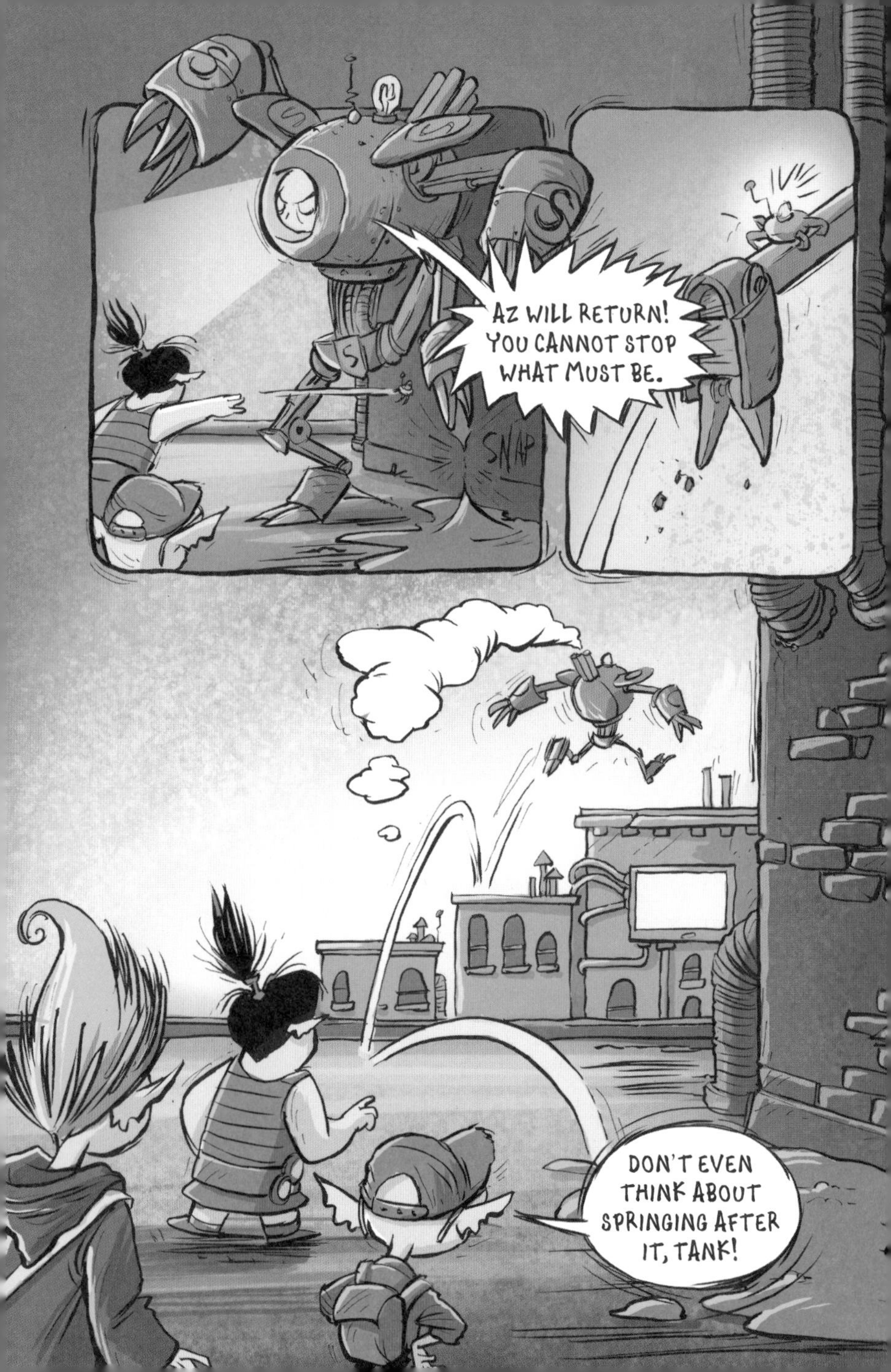
AZ WILL RETURN! YOU CANNOT STOP WHAT MUST BE.
SNAP
DON'T EVEN THINK ABOUT SPRINGING AFTER IT, TANK!

We watched the battle bot until it was just a speck in the distance.

More questions nagged at my detective brain. They spilled out in one frustrated breath.

"What was that thing? Who was controlling it? Where is it going?" I slumped to the cold rooftop. "Now we'll never know."

Tank's phone chirped out a single pinging noise. The screen showed a map with a glowing red dot. The dot moved across the map.

"That tracking bug I tossed at it will keep us up-to-date on where the bot is going."

Tank's phone pinged again.

"Interesting." Tank studied the map on her phone. "The bot is heading into the Overlook."

"That's where all the rich monsters live," Aleetha said. "Why is it going there?"

From the rooftop, we could see across the city to the large homes perched on the rocky cliff known as the Overlook. The exclusive neighborhood was home to some of the richest and most powerful monsters in Slick City. Business leaders, politicians and celebrities lived there. It was no place for bots on the run.

"Maybe that's where the monster controlling the bot is," I said.

"I hope you're wrong, Fizz." Tank held up her phone for us to see.

The flashing red light of Tank's tracker had stopped moving. The bot had arrived at its destination. My heart crawled down to my tail when I read the label identifying the building.

"Grimlock Manor," I said.

"Mayor Grimlock's home!" Aleetha said. "Mayor Grimlock is controlling that battle bot?"

The answer to her question lay high on the ledges of the Overlook. If we wanted to stop the Codex and his army, that's where we would have to go.

Suddenly, facing demons in a dark library didn't seem so scary anymore.

CHAPTER TEN

Crashing the Party

Music blasted from Grimlock Manor.

The place was lit up brighter than a glow-shroom forest. Long limousines drove through the front gates to the mayor's cliffside home. Kobolds in sleek suits, trolls in tiaras and spider-folk draped in jewelry were all ushered into the mayor's brightly lit home by wide-shouldered ogres in dark suits. Outside the gates, a pack of reporters snapped photos as the rich and famous monsters arrived.

None of them noticed the three of us across the road, hiding behind a clump of boulder bushes.

"Mayor Grimlock sure knows how to throw a party," Aleetha whispered.

"And he didn't invite us?" Tank said. She stood to get a better look. "Even the police got invitations."

Four police cars lined the road outside the mansion. Half a dozen cops stood around their cars, chatting and looking bored. My tail twitched at the sight of the officer in charge.

DETECTIVE HORDISH!

Detective Hordish wasn't a bad ogre. He was just a grumpy cop who didn't like detectives like me and Tank messing up his investigations. And by messing up, I mean solving. Right now, he looked extra grumpy. He probably wasn't happy to spend his evening babysitting wealthy monsters.

Aleetha peered over a boulder bush. "The police are just standing around. They're not checking any of the partygoers. It's as if they're waiting for something."

"If Hordish sees us, something will happen," I said. "He'll send us packing back to our parents."

"He won't have to pack you very far, Fizz." Tank pointed through the boulder bushes to the reporters. In the scrum of photographers stood a very familiar goblin reporter. "Your mom is here."

I curled down even farther. I wished for a whole field of boulder bushes to hide in.

"I told her I was doing homework at your house, Tank," I said. "If she catches us here, I won't be allowed out of our cave for a month!"

"Let's make sure she doesn't see you out here then," Aleetha said.

"We can't stay out here all night," Tank said. "The bot went into the mayor's mansion. And that's where we have to go if we want to find out who is controlling it."

"It's hopeless," I said. "The only way into the mansion is through those front gates, right past my mom and Detective Hordish."

"Good thing I brought along my homework." Aleetha held up a small glass jar. A bright purple cream glowed inside. "My latest assignment. It should help get us inside that party."

"Since when has homework been helpful?" I grumbled.

Tank held out her phone like a shield to protect her. "It's magic! I am not touching any magic."

"Then have fun out here," Aleetha said with a shrug. "And keep your voice down. We're hiding, remember?"

"What is it?" I said.

"Mage's secret." Aleetha rubbed a bit of the cream on her arm. "Okay, it's doppelgänger sweat mixed with crushed naggle root and spices to make it smell nice."

"Doppelgänger?" I said. "You mean those shape-shifters from the Depths?"

"Disgusting!" Tank said. "And it's magic. Two reasons not to touch this stuff."

"Relax, Tank," Aleetha said. "Just put a little on your wrist, like this. And wait."

She reached out to dab the purple cream on the troll's arm.

Tank pulled her arm back. "No way!"

"Tank, we need to get inside the party," I said. "And we'll need you with us."

I took the cream from Aleetha and put some on my arm.

"All right." Tank took the jar and rubbed some cream on her wrist. "But how is this stuff going to get us into the party?"

"Like this," Aleetha said. The lava elf's words rumbled like thunder, and her body sparkled.

Being an ogre was weird. Everything seemed smaller. My extra height gave me a different view of the world around me. It was like I was standing on a ladder, but I could walk at the same time. Inside I was still a goblin, but to anyone looking at me I was an ogre.

I wasn't sure Aleetha's disguise would work. I held my breath as we walked past my mom and the other reporters. I was sure she would recognize me. But she didn't look twice at a trio of waiters rushing to the mayor's party. No one paid any attention to us.

"They probably think we're just late for work," Aleetha whispered as we walked up the driveway and through the front door.

It was the same inside the party. None of the wealthy monsters even looked at us. We were just hired help. Monsters in the Overlook never paid attention to the hired help. Even though I was double my usual size, I could move through this party as if I were a tiny bug. But we still had to be careful. Bugs can get splattered.

The mayor's party was a who's-who of monster royalty. All the important ogres, goblins and trolls were there. Business tycoons, celebrities and politicians chatted, laughed and danced in Mayor Grimlock's massive home.

Aleetha led us to a quiet corner under the stairs leading to the back of the mansion.

"I do *not* like being an ogre," Tank said after she bumped into the corner of the wall. She was clearly having a hard time getting used to her added size. "This will wear off, right?"

"Sooner than you think," Aleetha said. "I'm not sure how long it'll last, but it won't be long. We'd better keep moving."

"Moving where?" I said. Now that we were inside the party with all the well-dressed monsters and fancy food, finding the monster who controlled the battle bot seemed impossible.

"I got us through the front door," Aleetha said. "I was hoping you two would come up with a plan."

A door along the nearest wall swung open. A troll in the same waiter's uniform as us stepped into the room. She carried a wide tray heaped with rolled-up pastries and skewers of steaming meat. The waiter strolled around the room, offering the treats to the partygoers.

The door opened again and another troll appeared. This one was much older, with a face that looked like it was chiseled from old rubble. He snarled when he spotted us.

"You three! Quit standing around," Rubble-Face barked. He grabbed me by the sleeve and pulled me back to the door, motioning for Aleetha and Tank to follow. "Get in here! I have a special job for you."

CHAPTER ELEVEN

Monster Mansion

The smells and sounds of a busy kitchen wafted over us as we stepped through the doorway. Chefs frantically prepared dishes. Waiters rushed in and out, carrying trays of food for the hungry guests.

The rubble-faced troll pointed to one of the many platters of pastries and other delicious snacks sitting on the counter.

"Grab one of those and follow me."

I froze. If we did anything other than pretend to be waiters, we would be thrown out on our tails.

The troll rolled his eyes and took a tray from the counter. He shoved it into my hands.

"Lazy ogres. Can't find good help these days." He glared at the three of us. "Follow me. Think you can handle that?"

He didn't wait for an answer and marched to the far side of the kitchen.

I looked at Tank and Aleetha. Tank shrugged her large ogre shoulders, and she and Aleetha each took a tray. Playing along was the only option.

The old troll led us out of the kitchen, up some stairs and through another set of doors. The music and laughter of the guests faded as we walked farther into Mayor Grimlock's mansion.

We didn't stop until the troll opened a set of heavy doors and led us into a dimly lit room. This area was set up for another party. A party within a party. A table with bowls of punch stood against one wall. Soft chairs and couches dotted the space. A massive TV glowed down on us from the corner. The far wall was made completely of glass. On the other side of the glass stood a wide balcony with a view of all of Slick City. About a dozen older and fatter monsters lounged in those soft chairs, watching that large TV. In the largest, most comfortable chair sat the mayor of Slick City.

"Mayor Grimlock," I said. My voice sounded much deeper in my ogre disguise.

"That's right, kid," Rubble-Face said. "You are his personal waiters for the night, got it? Give them whatever they want. Keep them happy with food. I'll check back later."

The old troll left without another word.

The mayor and his monster pals kept us busy serving food and fetching drinks. Just when I thought we would have to get more food from the kitchen, a chubby goblin rushed into the room and ran up to the mayor.

I recognized the goblin from the mayor's press conference. It was Rufus, the monster who tried to turn off the jumbo screen after the Codex hacked into it. He looked equally flustered now.

"Mr. Mayor, did you forget about our meeting?"

"I didn't forget, Rufus." Mayor Grimlock looked at the goblin as if he were a bug. "I decided I would rather celebrate the opening of Slurp Stadium than listen to your warnings of doom and gloom."

"But you must listen, Mayor Grimlock!" Rufus said. He held up a sheet of vizpaper for the mayor to see. "I have new evidence that proves the Codex's predictions will come true."

Mayor Grimlock jumped to his feet and turned on Rufus. "Do not mention that name!"

A dark-haired troll moved to the mayor's side and placed a hand on his shoulder.

"Don't get too excited, Mayor Grimlock. Remember to breathe."

Calm seemed to wash over the mayor. The troll's words had soothed his temper. I recognized that troll from the press conference too. My mom had called him Sanzin. He was in charge of SlurpCo Industries and was one of the monsters pressuring the mayor to build the stadium.

Rufus pushed his vizpaper in front of the mayor again.

"I have the plans for the stadium here," he said. "The support pillars for the retractable roof are placed in a way that matches exactly the diagram from the archives I showed you earlier."

"That's enough, Rufus." Sanzin led the mayor away from his assistant. "Mayor Grimlock has worked hard to get Slurp Stadium built. He deserves a night off from you."

Rufus danced around Sanzin to face the mayor again.

"Just take a closer look at these documents, Mr. Mayor. There are some very odd additions to the structure of the stadium."

Sanzin released Rufus from his grip. The purple jewel around the troll's neck glowed, as if powered by his anger. Rufus fell back like he'd seen a demon from the Depths. He scurried out of the room, still clutching his vizpaper.

The room was silent. No one knew where to look. The mayor's guests wore smiles that did little to hide their fear and confusion. Sanzin grinned as though nothing had happened. He turned to where we stood near the food table.

"You three! Don't just stand there. Bring us some more foo…"

Sanzin's voice trailed off. His eyes had become the size of dinner plates. The other monsters looked at us. Their awkward smiles vanished. Their jaws fell open, moving but making no sound.

Beside me, Tank was melting. Her ogre disguise dripped off her in a wave of sparkly magic.

Aleetha's disguise wasn't doing much better.

I caught our reflection in a big mirror on the wall. The ogre waiters were gone, replaced by a troll, an elf and a pint-sized goblin. Aleetha's magic had worn off.

"Intruders!" Mayor Grimlock barked. "Sanzin, deal with these uninvited guests!"

Sanzin calmly tapped commands into his phone. "Certainly, Mayor Grimlock. Now we'll see what a SlurpCo security bot can do."

The SlurpCo security bot, under Sanzin's control, stomped closer. Now I knew who had sent the bot to spy on us at the library. But why? The bot's massive claws would have me before I had the answer.

The screen on the wall hanging behind the monsters flashed with a blinding purple light. The battle-bot tournament on the screen buzzed away. It was replaced by a familiar face.

The Codex's image loomed over the room. All eyes turned to the screen and the mask staring out at the room. Even the security bot froze in midstep.

"Greetings, Mayor Grimlock," the Codex crooned. "Very sorry to crash your party. I have come to give you a final warning. Close Slurp Stadium or the Codex Army will strike!"

The mayor glared at the face on the screen.

"I will do what I please, Codex!" he shouted. "Get out of my house!"

"Very well, little mayor." The Codex's laugh rippled through the TV speakers. "Tomorrow you will hail me as a hero."

The lock on the balcony doors pulsed with a purple light, then quietly clicked. Tank turned one of the handles. It opened.

Someone had remotely unlocked the doors.

We hurried out to the mayor's balcony.

Our exit didn't go unnoticed.

"Those brats are getting away!" Mayor Grimlock shouted.

The security bot buzzed back to life and thundered after us.

The balcony was wide and empty. There was plenty of room to run, but nowhere to hide. We reached the far railing. The lights of Slick City spread out below us all the way to Fang Harbor.

Aleetha peered over the railing and pulled her head back quickly.

"Too high to jump," she said.

The security bot stomped closer.

Tank fumbled with her tool belt, searching for something. She pulled a small brass ball out of one of the pockets.

My stomach dropped like it had been tossed off the balcony.

"What are you doing, Tank?" I said.

"Saving our butts."

She tossed the ball into the air.

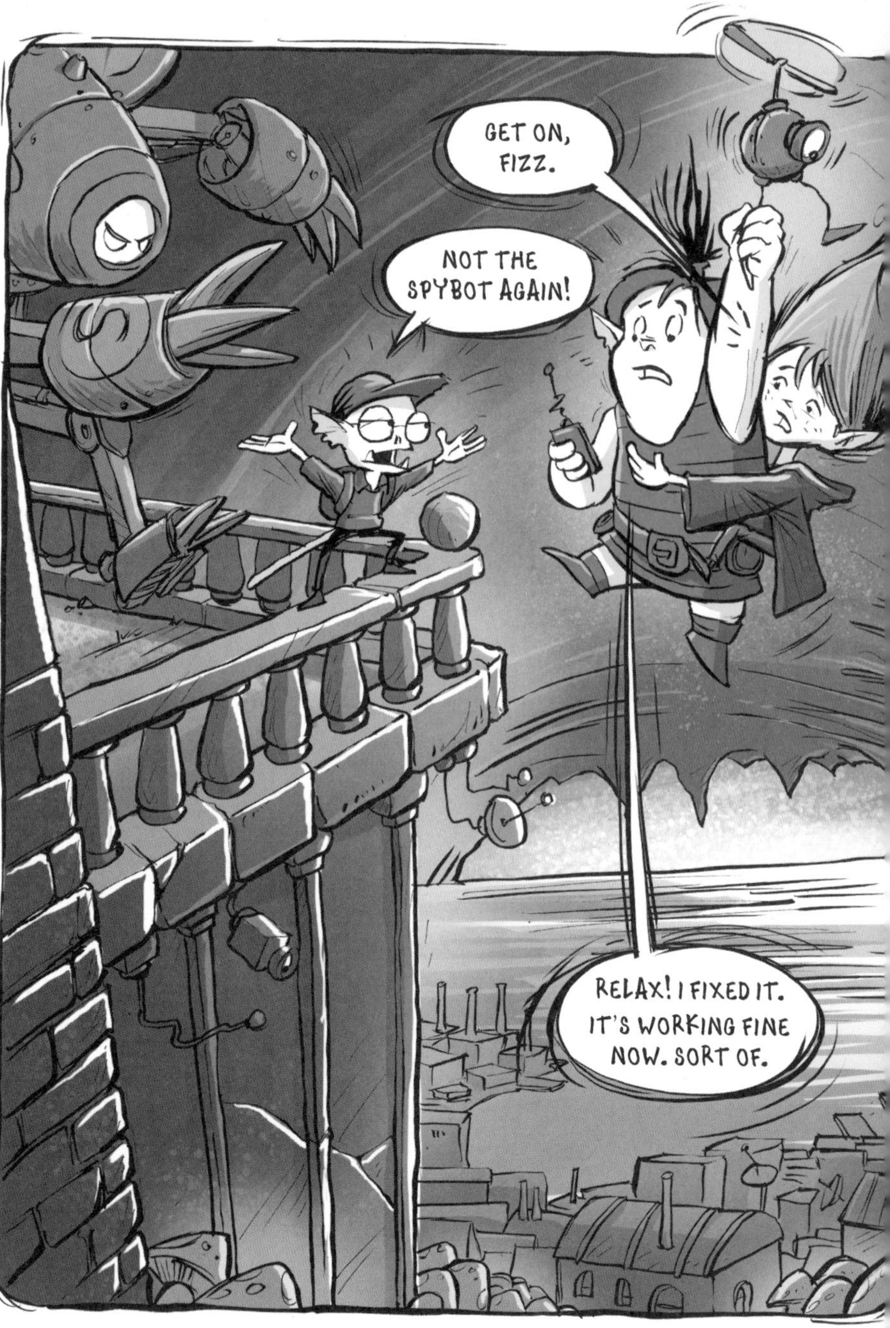
GET ON, FIZZ.
NOT THE SPYBOT AGAIN!
RELAX! I FIXED IT. IT'S WORKING FINE NOW. SORT OF.

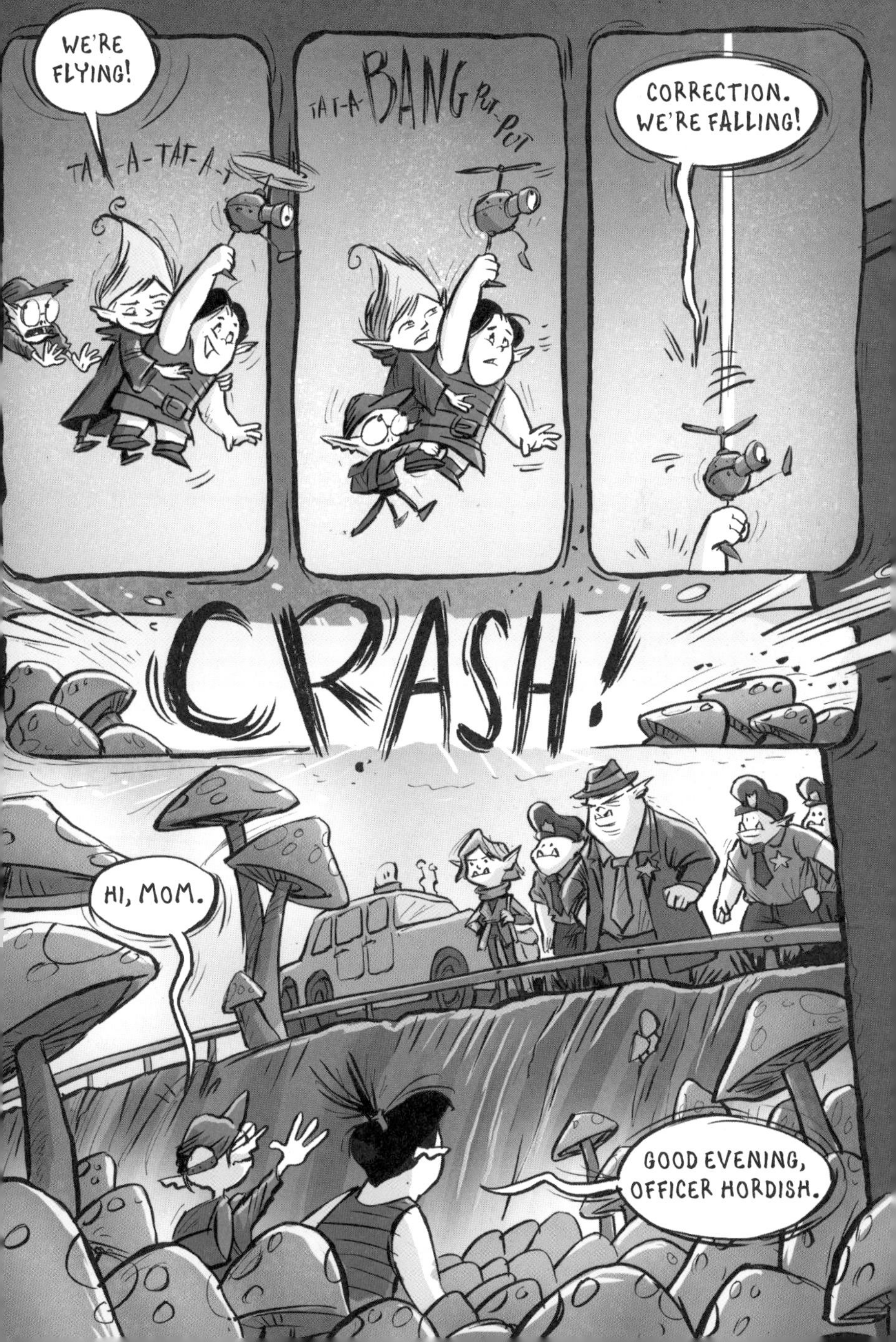
WE'RE FLYING!
TAT-A-TAT-A-T
TAT-A-BANG PUT-PUT
CORRECTION. WE'RE FALLING!
CRASH!
HI, MOM.
GOOD EVENING, OFFICER HORDISH.

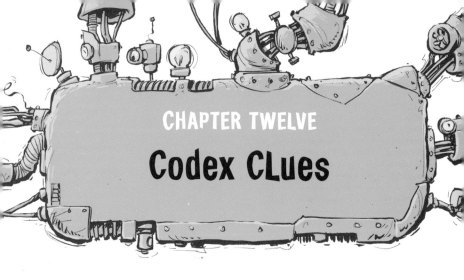

CHAPTER TWELVE
Codex CLues

The police van smelled like stale coffee. Or maybe it was just Detective Hordish.

The ogre police officer scowled at the three of us from the back door. We huddled together inside the van on a narrow bench, wrapped in itchy blankets. Mom was there too. From the way she chewed her fangs, I knew I was in trouble.

"I thought you were with Tank's family, doing homework," she said. "But it turns out you three were running around the mayor's mansion, disguised as waiters. I'm upset, Fizz."

"The mayor is very upset too," Hordish said.

"*He's* upset?" Aleetha jumped to her feet. "He nearly killed us with that security bot!"

Hordish scowled. "The mayor tells a different story. He thinks you are the Codex."

"What?"

"That's ridiculous," Mom said. "Just because the kids crashed his party doesn't mean they are the Codex."

"Just like how the kids crashed the mayor's press conference?" Hordish said. "When you little monsters show up, the Codex is never far behind. The mayor thinks that is suspicious. And I agree with him."

"It's a coincidence!" I said.

"Police officers don't believe in coincidences," Hordish said. "The mayor sent us here to watch out for the Codex. And then you three land right in our laps."

"It's more complicated than that," Aleetha said.

"Go on," Hordish said.

Aleetha's eyes met mine. I knew what she was thinking. She took a deep breath and started talking.

"It all started with this book we found in the library," she said.

Aleetha told my mom and Detective Hordish about the guardian in the book and about Az, the demon. She explained how the hacker known as the Codex was using the demon's face to scare the mayor. I added the bit about the ancient goblin map with the weird oval shape right where Slurp Stadium was built. And Tank told them about the security bot we'd chased along the rooftops.

Mom was silent while she digested the fact that her only son had nearly been eaten by a demon and a security bot in one night.

"And that troll Sanzin is the one controlling the battle bot!" Tank said. "He sent the bot to spy on us at the library."

"Slow down there, young troll," Detective Hordish said. "Sanzin Balazar runs the biggest company in Rockfall Mountain. Without SlurpCo Industries, there would be no jobs in Slick City. Sanzin is a leader. Watch what you say about him."

"He's a sneak and he's up to something." Tank crossed her arms and scowled at the floor of the van.

Detective Hordish tugged on the collar of his shirt. "There's a lot you're not thinking about. The mayor also claims you somehow opened the balcony doors after the whole mansion was in lockdown."

"We didn't do that!" Tank said. "They just unlocked themselves."

"Or you had help." Hordish smiled. "From a mysterious computer hacker terrorizing our city. If you aren't the Codex, then you are friends with the Codex. That makes you suspects."

My tail went into twitch overload. We came out here to solve the mystery of the Codex. Now, we were all suspects. The police thought we were the Codex. Detective Hordish was definitely wrong about that. But he raised a good point. Who had unlocked the doors to the balcony? Did the Codex help us escape?

My thoughts were shattered by a blinding flash of light coming from the mayor's house.

LOOKS LIKE THE MAYOR IS ENDING HIS PARTY WITH FIREWORKS.

I DON'T THINK THEY'RE HIS FIREWORKS, MOM.

POLICE

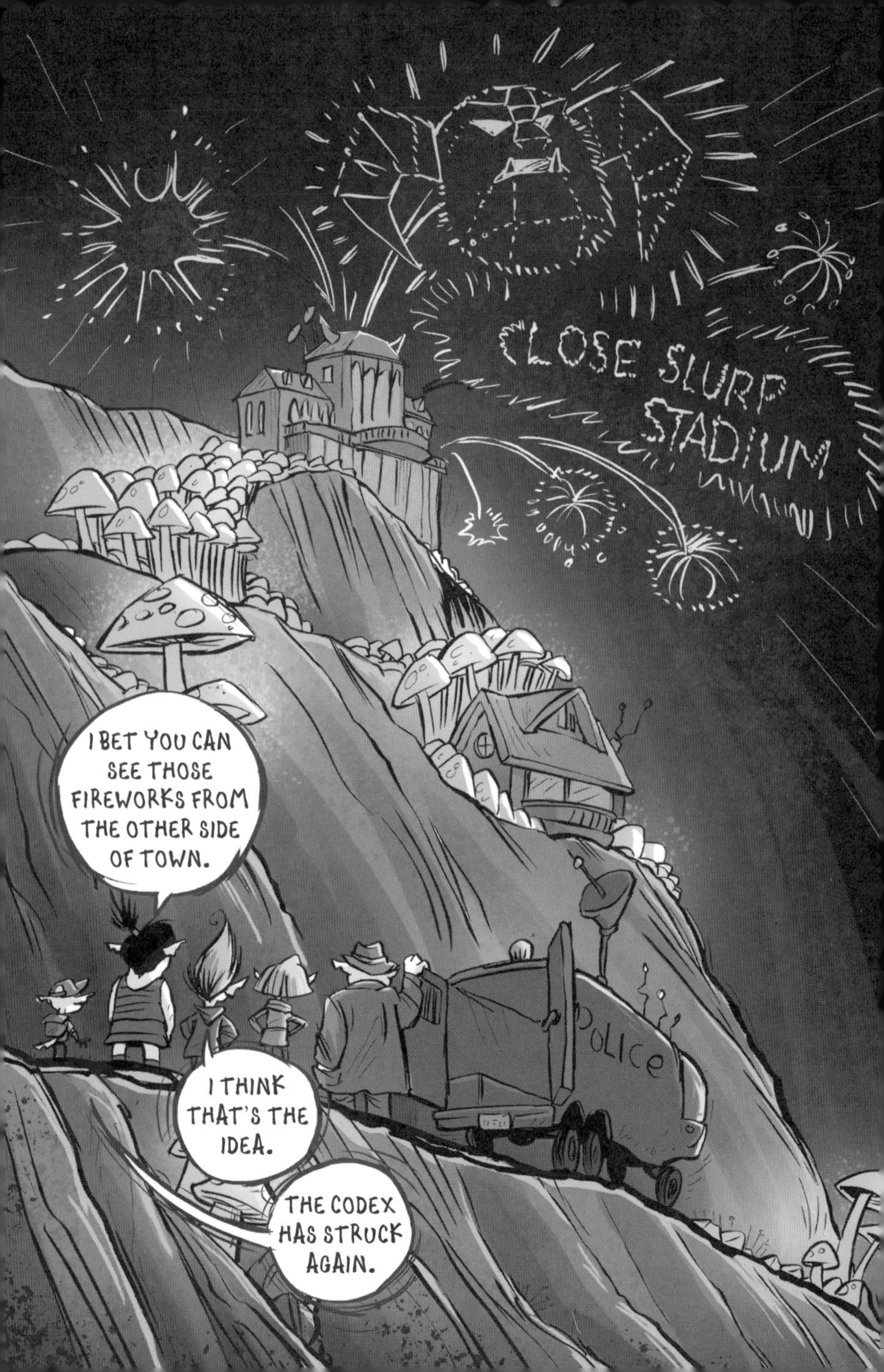
CLOSE SLURP STADIUM
I BET YOU CAN SEE THOSE FIREWORKS FROM THE OTHER SIDE OF TOWN.
I THINK THAT'S THE IDEA.
THE CODEX HAS STRUCK AGAIN.
POLICE

After the Codex's light show, Mom declared us officially off the case. Detective Hordish reluctantly agreed we weren't the Codex and let us go home. But the old ogre wasn't fully convinced we weren't wrapped up in this Codex mess. Mom told me to forget the hacker and focus on solving the Mystery of the Unfinished Homework piling up in my schoolbag.

The next day, she kept me within tail's reach like I was a toddler. It was the weekend, but I was stuck following her around town, getting groceries and a thousand other totally boring errands. The highlight was swinging by the Bouncing Bugbear for an end-of-shopping treat.

MOM, WHAT DO YOU KNOW ABOUT GOBLIN HISTORY?

NOT MUCH. YOUR GRANDPA USED TO TELL US OLD GOBLIN LEGENDS. BUT THEY WERE JUST STORIES TO SCARE US.

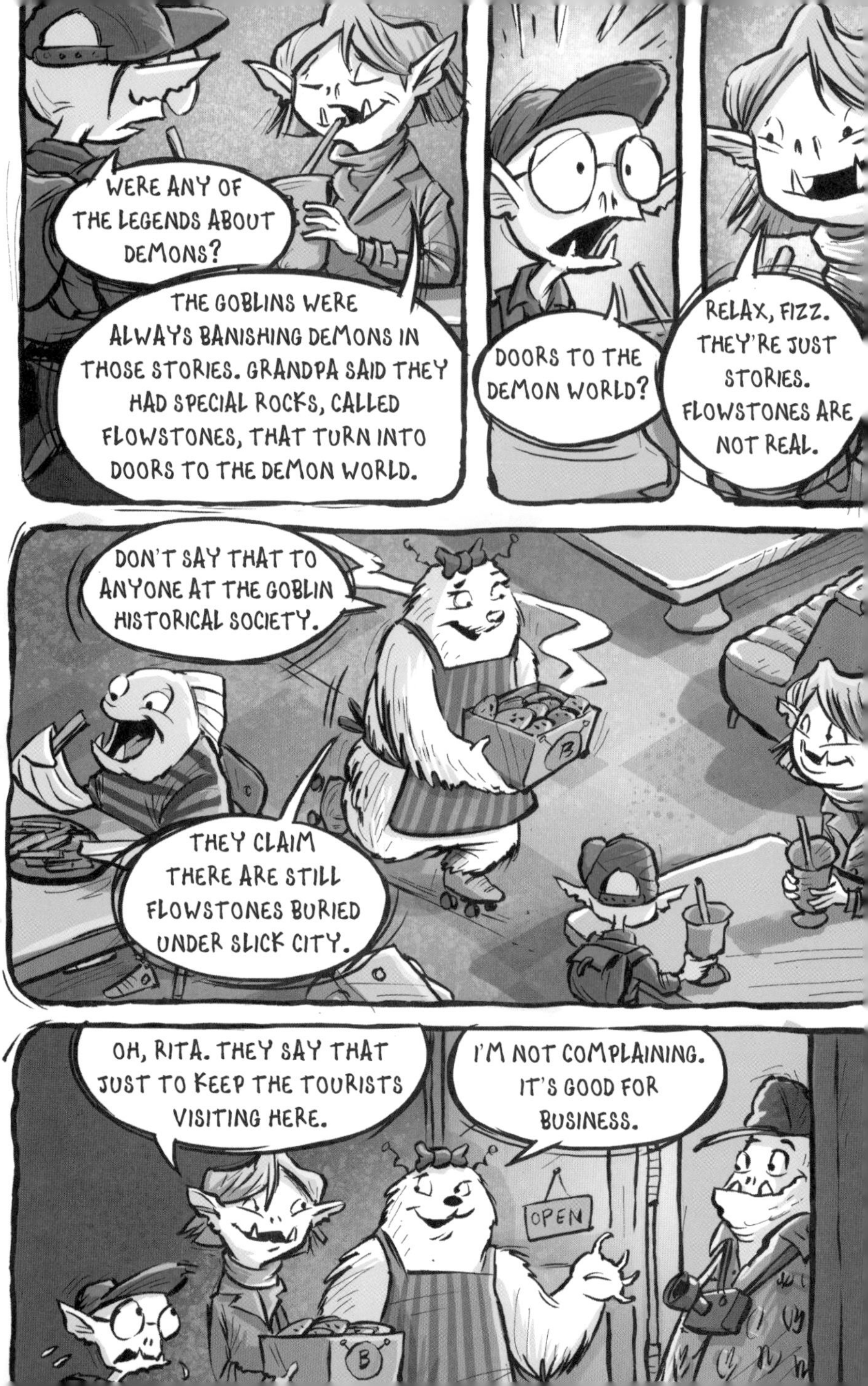
WERE ANY OF THE LEGENDS ABOUT DEMONS?
THE GOBLINS WERE ALWAYS BANISHING DEMONS IN THOSE STORIES. GRANDPA SAID THEY HAD SPECIAL ROCKS, CALLED FLOWSTONES, THAT TURN INTO DOORS TO THE DEMON WORLD.
DOORS TO THE DEMON WORLD?
RELAX, FIZZ. THEY'RE JUST STORIES. FLOWSTONES ARE NOT REAL.
DON'T SAY THAT TO ANYONE AT THE GOBLIN HISTORICAL SOCIETY.
THEY CLAIM THERE ARE STILL FLOWSTONES BURIED UNDER SLICK CITY.
OH, RITA. THEY SAY THAT JUST TO KEEP THE TOURISTS VISITING HERE.
I'M NOT COMPLAINING. IT'S GOOD FOR BUSINESS.
OPEN

Outside the café, Mom handed me the box of Rita's cookies.

"Take these to Tank," she said. "Her mom sent me a message. Tank has been in her workshop all morning and won't come out."

I took the box of cookies. They were still warm.

"She's sad because we're banned from investigating the Codex."

"Think about that next time you decide to jump off the mayor's balcony, Fizz." Mom's words were stern, but her eyes held a mischievous twinkle. "I'm not a fan of Mayor Grimlock, but I am a fan of keeping my little goblin in one piece. Got it?"

"Got it."

"Good. Let's catch our bus. You can drop by Tank's house. Cheer her up, but no more Codex snooping! Leave that to Detective Hordish."

Mom scratched the scales behind my ears, and I felt as warm as the cookies in the box.

Tank didn't even grunt hello when I came down the stairs into her workshop. Gadgets and gear were spread all through the small basement room. Wires, diodes and doodads covered her workbench. It was a tinkering troll's paradise, but Tank looked sadder than a slime with no garbage to eat. She sat hunched over, silently poking a screwdriver at a damaged circuit board.

I slid the box of cookies across her workbench.

"Have one," I said. "Rita baked them just for you. They won't help us solve this mystery, but they will cheer you up."

My best friend took a cookie and munched in silence. I took one and joined her in quiet chewing.

This whole case had started out with Rizzo Rawlins and his illegal battle-bot parts. Now we were wrapped up in a battle between the mayor of Slick City and a mysterious hacker known only as the Codex.

My mom and Detective Hordish might have wanted us off the case, but that wasn't happening. Unsolved cases are like itches that must be scratched. And Tank and I weren't done scratching.

"The Battle Bot Cup is tonight, Fizz," Tank said. The cookies must have helped her find her voice. "And we still haven't proven Rizzo is cheating."

"True, but if we don't stop the Codex from his big hack tonight, it won't matter what parts Rizzo has running in his battle bot."

"How can we stop the Codex? The cops have no idea who he is or what he is planning to do," Tank said. "I'll be happy if we can bust Rizzo for cheating and have the Troll Patrol represent Gravelmuck in tonight's battle."

"Is that why you're still looking at those spybot photos?"

Images from our disastrous snooping with the spybot covered the large screen hanging above Tank's workbench. I had looked at the photos a dozen times. There were pictures of Rizzo and the Gutro twins talking to the Codex on the billboard, and photos of Rizzo with the strange equipment that even the Troll Patrol guys couldn't identify.

"I know it's useless, but I don't know what else to do," she said. "These photos don't prove Rizzo is cheating. We need a picture of the Codex's equipment actually inside Rizzo's battle bot."

"And that's not going to happen," I said. "We tried that already, remember."

Tank scrolled through the photos on the screen. The spybot had taken a lot of pictures. Most of them were of the ground or the buildings around the parking lot where Rizzo had met the Codex.

One photo jumped out at me.

"Scroll back," I said. Tank rolled the photos back across the screen until I saw the one that had caught my eye. "There. Zoom in on that one."

"The spybot was just warming up when it took this one, Fizz. It's nothing."

"Wrong," I said. "It's definitely something, and it's been staring at us the whole time."

It was a photo taken from very high in the air, showing the parking lot. Rizzo and the twins were just dots on the ground. But, across the street, the image showed something else: Slurp Stadium.

The stadium looked totally different seen from that high in the air. Its retractable roof was open. I could see right down to the battle-bot field. Except there wasn't a field. It was a giant hole. Slurp Stadium had a retractable field as well as a retractable roof.

In the hole was something I had seen before.

My tail twitched like it was swatting at a swarm of nipticks. Pieces of the puzzle were falling into place, but I didn't like what I was beginning to see.

"We need to talk to Aleetha," I said. "I think I know why the Codex wants Slurp Stadium closed. And I hope I'm wrong."

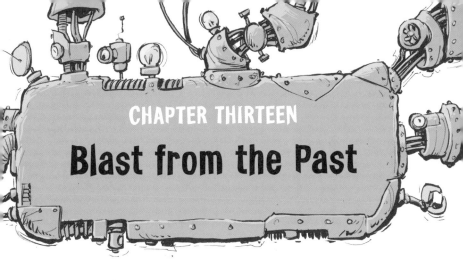

CHAPTER THIRTEEN

Blast from the Past

Slurp Stadium was bursting with monsters.

Every troll, goblin and ogre in Slick City had come here to be part of the grand opening celebrations. Music blasted from loudspeakers. Smells from the food vendors wafted through the air. Crowds of monsters gawked at the new stadium and watched young coders showing off their battle-bot skills in the battle-bot playground.

The playground was a big open area in the stadium, just outside the actual battle-bot arena. Battle bots were everywhere, running, jumping, flying and buzzing in the air. Every battle-bot team that hadn't made the finals was here. But only a few lucky teams would compete in tonight's battle.

The opening party had begun, but we had no reason to celebrate. We still had no idea what the Codex had planned with his army, and we were no closer to proving Rizzo was a cheat. We found the Troll Patrol putting their bot, Thrasher, through an obstacle course. The bot looked good, but our troll friends were in no mood to celebrate.

"Somebody needs to teach that kobold a lesson," Ryla growled after Rizzo had left.

"I think it's too late for that," said Zarkof. "Rizzo has everyone fooled. All we can do is sit back and try to enjoy the show."

"I'm not ready to sit back," I said. "And the only thing I want to enjoy is watching Rizzo get busted."

Daztan arched a bushy eyebrow. "You two have a plan?"

"Calling it a plan is a stretch," Tank said. "Just keep your bot batteries charged and ready for battle."

"We'll be ready," Ryla said with a wide grin.

Tank was right. We didn't have a plan. I'd mashed together a few ideas on how to stop the Codex and reveal Rizzo as a cheat. Before that mash-up of ideas could become a plan, we needed to find Aleetha.

The wizards' work area was easy to spot. It was the only one popping with magic. The telltale sparkle of spells floated in the air around their bot, like smoke rising from a fire.

"I still don't think it's fair that the Shadow Tower gets to compete," Tank said.

"You heard Aleetha, Tank. Their battle bots are the same. They're just powered with magic instead of computer code."

"It's still creepy," she said.

"Keep that to yourself," I said. "There are enough battles going on tonight without adding magic versus technology to the list."

I spotted Aleetha with the wizards' bot crew. Four lava elves in long dark robes huddled around their battle bot. I could see flashes of the bot as the mages moved around it.

"Their bot looks totally normal to me," I said.

Tank snorted. "It's not the bot, Fizz. It's how they make the bot work. Do you notice they have no tools? No wrenches or hammers or even circuit boards. Never trust a bot builder that has no tools, Fizz."

"They just do things differently." I sighed. "They use magic instead of tools. If you ask me, technology is as dangerous as magic. Just look at what the Codex has done so far."

Before Tank could answer, Aleetha ran up to us. She took us each by an arm and led us away from the wizards tinkering with the bot.

"We better talk over here. My friends don't trust trolls and their tech."

I shot Tank a "don't say anything" look that, thankfully, she understood.

"Did you bring it?" I asked, quickly changing the topic.

She nodded. "I got your message."

We found a spot away from the running, jumping bots. Aleetha pulled a long scroll from her bag and spread it on the ground.

"Is that the map from the library? The one from the time before the ogres arrived?" Tank asked.

"It's a copy," Aleetha said. "I ordered one from the library after our little adventure in the map room."

I studied the old goblin map. All around Fang Harbor was an open field of glowshrooms and boulder bushes. Goblins had lived along the water's edge, catching haggle fish and harvesting mushrooms. No roads, no buildings and no Slurp Stadium. But there was that one thing marked on the map. And it was exactly what I was looking for.

"Tank, give me your phone," I said.

I scrolled through Tank's photos. My tail tingled when I found the one I needed.

There was no denying it. The shape on the goblin map matched the shape in the ground under the stadium. I had no idea what that meant, but it got my tail wagging.

"We're finally getting closer to figuring out what the Codex is up to," I said.

"Don't start your victory dance just yet, Fizz," Aleetha said. "It's not all good news."

She pulled another scroll from her robes and unrolled it on the ground beside the map.

"That's the page from the goblin history book," Tank said. "The one you showed us at the library."

Aleetha ran her hand along the stick-figure drawing of the goblin.

"I finally found a teacher at school who would help me translate the words from ancient goblin," she said. Her voice went quiet as she spoke. "It is a set of instructions."

Tank looked up from the map. "Instructions? For what?"

"I don't know. The teacher could only recognize some of the words. Ancient goblin isn't a popular subject in the Shadow Tower." Aleetha glanced at me. "Sorry, Fizz."

"No worries." I shrugged. "Magic isn't a popular subject at Gravelmuck Elementary."

"Very true." Aleetha grinned. She turned back to the page on the ground. "My teacher did recognize the shapes on the page and map. She called them flowstones."

"Flowstones?" I said, remembering my chat with Mom at the Bouncing Bugbear Café. "I thought flowstones weren't real."

"They are very real and very powerful," Aleetha said.

My brain puzzled through it all. If the shape on the map was a flowstone, and it matched the shape in Tank's photo, that could only mean one thing. "There is a flowstone buried under Slurp Stadium," I said.

"So what?" Tank said. She stared at the map. Her ears drooped like they always did when she was working out a difficult math problem. "What's so special about a bunch of rocks?"

Aleetha looked over her shoulder. Around us, the battle-bot preparations carried on. Technicians fine-tuned their contraptions, and battle-bot fans checked out the new machines. No one paid any attention to three kids in a quiet corner, huddled around an old map. Convinced no one was listening, Aleetha leaned in close.

"When activated, a flowstone can be transformed," she said.

"Transformed into what?" Tank said.

"A gateway to the world of demons," Aleetha said.

"Demons?" Tank said. "Like Az?"

"Az will return," I whispered. "That's what the guardian said at the library, before we sent it back into its book."

"It makes sense," Tank said. "The flowstones on the goblin map, in the history book and in the photo match. They are all connected to this stadium."

"That's because Slurp Stadium isn't just a stadium," I said. The scattered pieces of the puzzle snapped into place. "It's a gateway to the world where Az the demon is trapped."

Tank's ears snapped to attention on her head. "The Codex Army!" she said. "Remember how he talked about bringing his army to life? Codex is going to use the flowstone under Slurp Stadium to bring Az the demon back to Rockfall Mountain. That's what he's planning for tonight!"

Around us the battle-bot preparations continued. Monsters of all shapes and sizes were gearing up for a night of action. Little did they know what was really in store for them.

"A demon like Az would destroy Slick City," Aleetha said.

I gulped. "I think that's the idea."

CHAPTER FOURTEEN
The Battle Begins

Finding out your town's new battle-bot arena is actually a gate for releasing an ancient demon is enough to turn anyone off sports.

"We have to stop the battle-bot tournament," I said. "We have to tell someone."

"Who is going to believe us, Fizz?" Aleetha said.

"We could try Detective Hordish again," Tank said. "I saw the police earlier outside the stadium entrance."

"Where are they now? The police could stop the tournament," Aleetha said. She rolled up the map and history-book page and tucked them into the folds of her wizard's robe. "It's a long shot, but it could work."

It was a really long shot. Hordish thought we were behind the Codex hoaxes. Now we had to convince him to shut down the biggest event in the city's newest stadium to stop the Codex.

"Let's find our old friend Detective Hordish," I said.

Tank led the way through the crowd. We hadn't gotten very far when the speakers around the stadium buzzed to life.

"Attention, battle-bot fans! Find your seats. The action is about to begin!"

A horde of monsters hurried to their seats. Trolls, goblins and ogres all moved in the same direction. Unfortunately, it was the opposite of the way we were heading. We pushed against the crowd, but we didn't get far. We were like three haggle fish swimming upstream.

"We'll never find Hordish in time!" Aleetha shouted over the pre-battle noise.

She was right. In the crush of monsters, we would never find the detective or any other Slick City police officer. All I could see were eager battle-bot fans making their way to their seats. And one lone goblin on the edge of the crowd, quietly moving along the wall and away from the battle-bot arena.

The mayor's assistant had tried to warn Mayor Grimlock about the stadium. Did he know about the flowstone underneath the playing field? Maybe if we showed Rufus the map, he could convince the mayor to stop the tournament in time. The chance of that happening was fatter than the mayor himself, but with no cops around, it was all we had.

"Change of plan," I shouted.

We got to the edge of the crowd just as Rufus slipped through a door labeled *Employees Only*. I pushed my way to the door, with Aleetha and Tank at my tail. It was unlocked. Finally, a little luck to go with my long shots and fat chances.

We slipped through the door. A narrow passage led up to the top of the stadium. There was no sign of Rufus.

Halfway up the stairs, the wall gave way to a large window overlooking the battle-bot arena below.

The first battle was already underway. The Rawlins Reaper faced off against a battle bot with a snake's head and metal fangs. It looked like it could be a fair fight, except Rizzo's bot moved like a ramped-up zip beetle. Snake Head could hardly keep up with the Reaper's movements. My scales bristled at the sight of the cheating kobold.

"Easy, Fizz," Tank said, trying to pull me away from the window. "We'll deal with Rizzo another day."

"Right now, we have a demon to stop," Aleetha said.

The crowd below us cheered. Rizzo's Reaper had Snake Head on its back. It looked like the fight was over for the snake bot. Before Rizzo could deliver the final blow, the lights went out. The entire stadium was plunged into darkness.

The jumbo screen hanging over the middle of the arena lit up the darkness. The purple glow from the screen cast eerie shadows across the confused monsters in their seats. My anger at Rizzo vanished when the face of the Codex appeared on the screen.

"Greetings, Slick City!" the Codex's voice boomed over the stadium's speakers. "Mayor Grimlock, I warned you not to open this stadium."

"Oh no," Tank said. "We're too late."

All around the stadium, the monsters were stunned into silence.

"You have had plenty of time to listen to me, Slick City!"

My ears perked up when the Codex spoke. His words blasted through the stadium speakers, but they also came from somewhere close by.

Without a word, I moved silently along the narrow corridor. Tank and Aleetha followed. Together, we quietly climbed another set of stairs and came to the end of the corridor.

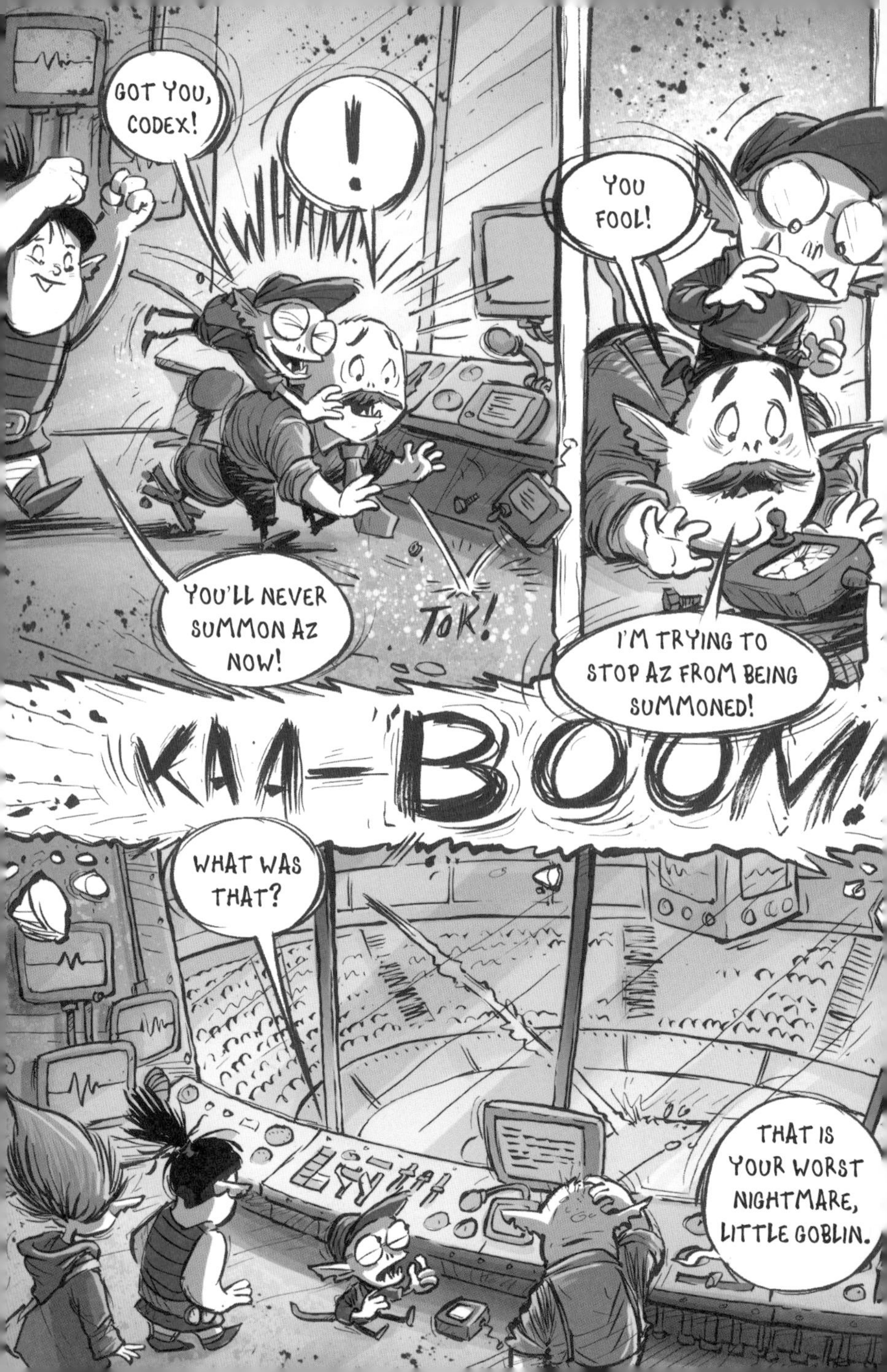
GOT YOU, CODEX!
!
WHAM
YOU'LL NEVER SUMMON AZ NOW!
TOK!
YOU FOOL!
I'M TRYING TO STOP AZ FROM BEING SUMMONED!
KAA-BOOM!
WHAT WAS THAT?
THAT IS YOUR WORST NIGHTMARE, LITTLE GOBLIN.

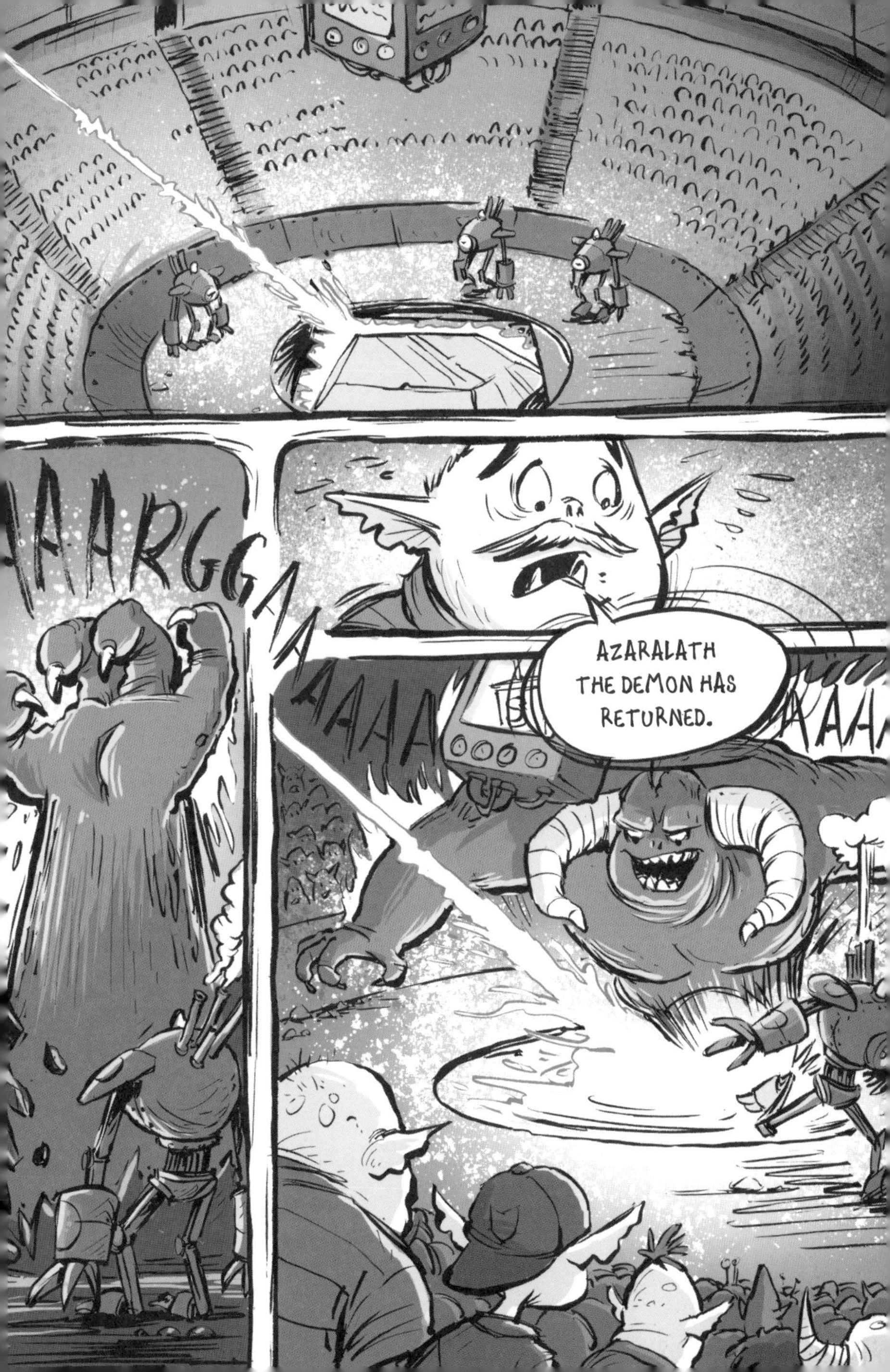
HAARGGAAAAAA
AZARALATH THE DEMON HAS RETURNED.
AAAA

CHAPTER FIFTEEN

Playing Nice with Demons

You know that feeling you get when you try to stop a demon from being summoned but accidentally help summon it? It definitely takes the shine off your scales.

When Az climbed through the flowstone, most monsters in the crowd thought it was part of the show. They cheered at the battle to come. When Az started smashing holes in the walls of the battle arena, the cheers turned to screams. After that, everything was a mess.

As Az stomped around the arena, smashing the walls and tearing down pillars, monsters of all sizes scrambled for the exits.

We watched the destruction unfold through the window overlooking the arena. I was mad, but mostly at myself. Rufus was the Codex. He wasn't planning to summon the demon. He was trying to stop the demon from being summoned.

"Why didn't you just warn the mayor?" I said.

"I did!" Rufus snapped. "I told him over and over again. Do you think he'd listen to me? No way! What did I know? I'm just a dumb goblin."

"A goblin who knows his history," Tank said.

"Exactly," Rufus said. He stomped away from the window and picked up the piece of equipment I had knocked from his hands when I tackled him. He turned it over, checking it for damage. "No one cares about history, so we are doomed to repeat it. Our ancestors used the flowstones to banish the demons. Now, all the tech-loving monsters don't even believe flowstones are real!"

"I believe they are real," I said.

Rufus looked up from the circuit board.

"It's a little late," he said. "I invented the Codex to get the mayor's attention. Even then, the big oaf wouldn't listen. He was more interested in building a big shiny sports stadium with SlurpCo's money."

Slurp Stadium was no longer shiny. Az the demon was seeing to that. Another crash of falling rocks echoed across the stadium.

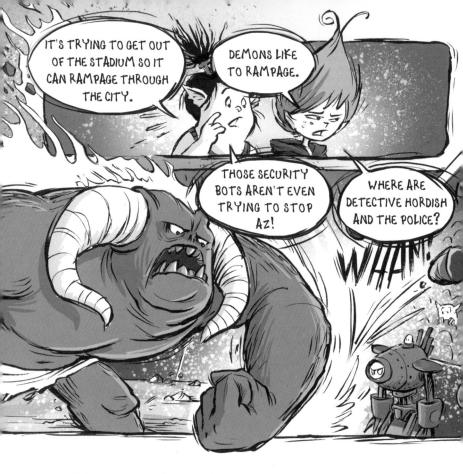

Tank was right. In the whole stadium, there wasn't a single Slick City police officer. It was as if Detective Hordish's whole department had decided to take a bathroom break. Talk about bad timing.

Rufus laughed at Tank's question. He worked at the circuit board with a pair of small pliers, trying to bend it back into shape.

"The police aren't even allowed in the stadium," he said. "SlurpCo insisted its own bots run security for these events."

"That's why we couldn't find them!" I said.

"Why would the police agree to being kept out of the stadium?" Aleetha said.

"They didn't," Rufus said. "Mayor Grimlock ordered them to stay out."

Aleetha wasn't convinced. "Why would he do that?"

"Because Sanzin from SlurpCo told him to," Rufus said. "Mayor Grimlock does whatever that troll tells him to."

"If the SlurpCo security bots are in charge, why aren't they stopping Az?" I said.

Rufus shrugged. "Who knows? Maybe they're waiting for orders?"

"We don't have time to wait," I said. "We have to do something."

I had no idea what that something should be, but I knew it had to be done.

"I *am* doing something," Rufus said. "I'm learning that you broke my remote bot compiler when you tackled me."

"Remote what?" I said.

Rufus held up a twisted circuit board with crooked wires dangling off one side.

"The remote bot compiler. It was the key to stopping Az from eating Slick City. Then you decided to jump on me like we were playing mudball." He tossed the compiler to the ground. "Now it will make a fine paperweight."

I didn't think I could feel any worse. Slick City was going to be destroyed, and it was all my fault. I wanted to jump through the flowstone and never come back.

"It's hopeless," I said.

"Pretty much," Rufus said.

"That doesn't mean we stop trying." Aleetha stood by the window, watching as Az smashed the stadium below.

"It's no use. Once Az is out of the stadium, he'll tear up Slick City," I said. "It will take all the wizards in the Shadow Tower to stop him. If they even can."

"Or maybe just a few brave monsters," Rufus said.

"What are you talking about?" I said.

"You destroyed the remote bot compiler, but that doesn't mean you can't compile the bots manually."

"Me?" I said. "I don't even know what any of that means."

"You don't have to," Rufus said. "You just have to find that Rawlins brat and his battle bot. Inside that machine is the manual bot compiler. Turn it on and we have a chance."

Tank's ears perked up at the mention of Rizzo Rawlins.

"Why does Rizzo have a manual bot compiler in his battle bot?" she said.

"He doesn't know that's what he has." Rufus's tail wagged back and forth faster than a sugared-up zip lizard. "The switch is buried inside the battle-bot processor unit the Codex gave him."

"The one he fished from the garbage earlier this week?" Tank said.

"The very one," Rufus said.

"I knew Rizzo was cheating!" I said.

I jumped to high-five Tank's waiting hand. Finally, we had proof that Rizzo had the Codex's processor in his battle bot. Another roar from Az erupted from the arena floor and cut our celebration short.

More screams from fleeing monsters followed the roar, but I wasn't scared anymore. We were right about Rizzo cheating. We had tracked down the Codex. If the cops and SlurpCo guards weren't going to stop the demon, then we would do that too. Somehow.

"All right, I'll do it," I said. "Tell us what we have to do."

Rufus laid out his plan. We didn't like any of it. Not a single word.

But it didn't matter what we thought. If we wanted to save Slick City, we were going to have to get real close to Az the demon.

We crept along the stadium seats, high above Az and his wall smashing.

"He's nearly through the wall," Tank said. "If we don't get down to the arena floor soon, we'll never stop him from destroying the city."

"The stairs aren't far," Aleetha said. "Keep moving."

Ahead of us, a narrow set of stairs ran all the way down to the front-row seats. The plan was to hurry down those, hop over the fence, and save the day. It was a little light on details, but it's hard to plan when there's a demon hammering the walls around you.

The stadium shook with another smash from Az. Only a few more strikes and he would be through that wall and free to take the carnage on the road. All the action was down on the arena floor, but something small and shiny above us caught my attention.

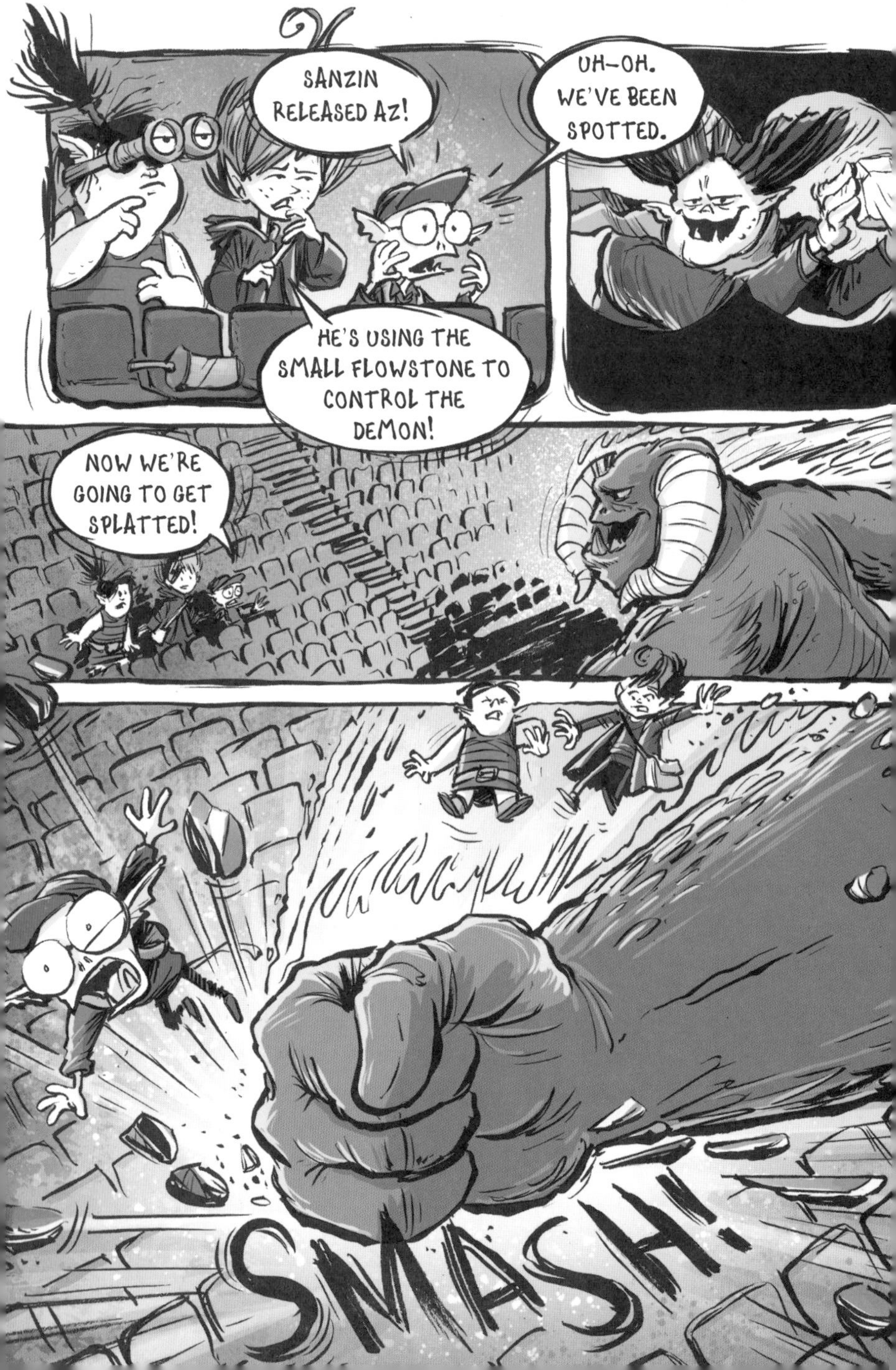

SANZIN RELEASED AZ!
HE'S USING THE SMALL FLOWSTONE TO CONTROL THE DEMON!
UH-OH. WE'VE BEEN SPOTTED.
NOW WE'RE GOING TO GET SPLATTED!
SMASH!

Everything hurt. Getting smashed and thrown through the air by a demon will do that to you, I guess.

I crash-landed on the arena floor and lay there for what felt like a very long time. Eventually, things came into focus.

The floor was covered in busted battle-bot parts and smashed pieces of the stadium. There was no sign of Tank or Aleetha. My scales burned at the thought of them being under one of those piles of stone. I wanted to run and search for them, but Az had beaten me to it. The demon picked through the rubble near the spot he had just smashed. He was looking for survivors, but he wasn't planning on kissing their boo-boos better.

If Tank and Aleetha were under that pile, I had to find another way to help them.

Not far from my landing spot lay the crushed frame of the Rawlins Reaper. Rizzo's battle bot had not survived Az's attack. Next to the destroyed battle bot lay an equally crushed snarkdog vendor's cart. The cart's colorful awning was spread across the ground like a picnic blanket. A furry and familiar tail stuck out from under the awning.

I scrambled to my feet and ran for the cart. All the pain from my fall vanished at the opportunity lying in front of me. I threw back the awning.

"Get out from under there, Rizzo," I said.

The kobold jumped when he saw me.

"Is it gone? Don't let it get me!" Rizzo's fur stood on end, and his snout was covered in tears.

The big bully was crying. Normally, I'd take a bit of pleasure in this, as payback for all the noogies, wedgies and scale-scrapes he had given me. Right now, there wasn't time. I got down to business.

"Open your bot, Rizzo. I need to see what's underneath."

Even with the tears, the whimpering and the demon smashing up the place, Rizzo was defiant.

"No way, Fizzle!" he barked. "That's my bot. Only I can open it. Besides, I ain't running any illegal equipment."

Do bullies ever take a day off? Something inside me snapped. Maybe it was the guardian in the library, or my flying off Mayor Grimlock's balcony on Tank's spybot. Or maybe it was the fact that Tank and Aleetha could be smushed for all I knew. Whatever it was, I'd had enough of schoolyard bullies like Rizzo Rawlins.

I grabbed Rizzo by his tail and dragged him out from under the awning.

"Listen here, Rizzo," I snarled. "I know you took equipment from the Codex. I know that equipment is inside this battle bot. I know it makes your bot move faster than any other bot in the competition. I know you cheated. But I also know that doesn't matter anymore. What matters is that we stop that demon. Open this battle bot. Right now!"

Rizzo gulped. His ears flattened against his head.

"Okay, Fizz. Calm down. You only had to ask."

He pawed his access code into the bot's case. A hatch popped open with a faint hiss to reveal the circuitry underneath. I didn't understand half of it, but it looked impressive.

I searched the wires and circuits for the button Rufus had told me about. I found it quickly. The manual bot compiler. I had no idea what it did. But Rufus insisted it was our only chance, and I wasn't too picky at this point.

"What are you doing?" Rizzo whined.

"I'm saving your furry behind."

I reached out to press the button.

And was yanked back by my tail.

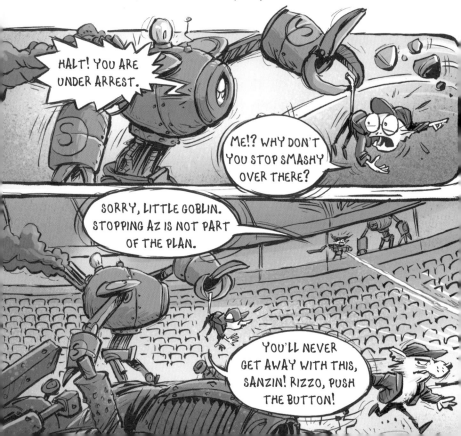

"Finish him!" Sanzin shouted.

Immediately, Az stopped searching the rubble and turned to face me. The demon responded to Sanzin's command and stomped closer. The arena shook with every step.

"I will enjoy watching you play with my demon," Sanzin called down from the safety of the SlurpCo box seats. "But don't take too long. I still have to help Mayor Grimlock spin this 'demon on a rampage' disaster into a triumph for rebuilding Slick City. With help from the SlurpCo construction company, of course."

"You're destroying Slick City just so your construction company can rebuild it?" I struggled against the security bot's tight grip, but it was no use.

149

"Pretty much," Sanzin said. "And there's the whole 'having a demon at your command' thing. That will come in handy, when SlurpCo Industries expands beyond Slick City."

With Az only a few demon steps away, the security bot let me go and hurried away to safety. The demon stomped closer. He raised one massive foot into the air above me. I scrambled away just as the foot smashed into the spot where I had stood only a second before. The ground exploded in a spray of rock and battle-bot pieces. I flew with them. For the second time in the longest day of my life, I crashed to the ground with a painful splat.

Az might be a good smasher and stomper, but he had terrible eyesight. After crushing the ground into rock salad, the demon stomped around the arena looking for me. He tossed aside broken chunks of stadium and bent battle-bot pieces as he looked for his little goblin playmate.

Az was playing the fist-smashing game, but I was playing hide-and-seek. And I was a good hider. When you're the size of a toadstool and have a bully like Rizzo Rawlins for a classmate, hiding becomes one of those must-have skills. The dented chest piece of a battle bot kept me out of sight and gave me time to think.

This was all Rizzo's fault. If that stubborn kobold hadn't argued with me, I would have had plenty of time to press the manual bot-compiler button before Sanzin's security bots nabbed me.

I wished Tank and Aleetha were with me. I hadn't seen them since Az's first fist-smash into the stadium seats. Were they under one of the piles of rubble? My scales tightened at the thought of them injured or worse. My whole body ached from my falls.

It was over. I was alone, trapped and hunted by a near-sighted but big-fisted demon. It was no use. I might as well give myself up and hope that Sanzin would just let me go back home. He could destroy Slick City if he wanted to. What did I care? Without my friends, the city meant nothing to me.

I peered out from under the dented chest piece. I couldn't see Az, but I could see the Rawlins Reaper lying on the ground not too far away. The bot's case had cracked open. The manual bot-compiler button was visible, screaming to be pushed.

The button also screamed of hope. Hope that Rufus's plan might work. Hope that Az could be stopped by the Codex's Army.

I shook aside my own misery and ran for Reaper.

The ground flew under my feet. I had never moved so fast. Visions of me trying out for the track team ran through my head. Weird, I know. But I had been knocked around a lot, so I blamed it on that. The button was within reach. Maybe I could do this. I dove through the air, my arm outstretched, ready to hit the bot-compiler button.

If I hadn't actually been there, dangling by my tail above that no-good kobold, I wouldn't have believed what I saw.

Rizzo Rawlins ran through the legs of the startled demon and into the middle of the arena.

"What are you doing?" I shouted.

"The thing you couldn't do, Fizzle!"

The kobold dove onto his busted battle bot and slammed his paw down on the bot-compiler button.

At first nothing happened. Then everything happened at once.

Pieces of Rizzo's broken battle bot began to glow bright purple. The glowing pieces floated into the air. So did the pieces of the Reaper's former opponent, the snake-head bot. Energy pulsed between the pieces of the broken battle bots. They floated closer and snapped together with a satisfying click.

More battle bot pieces floated into the arena, as if they were pulled by a powerful magnet. Each piece had the same purple glow and drifted toward the Reaper's chest piece. I recognized part of the Troll Patrol's Thrasher as it tumbled past and snapped onto the Reaper.

Az the demon was as confused as I was. Even Sanzin, filled with bravado only seconds earlier, was stunned into silence. Battle bots from every competitor flew into the arena, all zooming to the same spot: the manual compiler button on Rizzo's battle bot. The battle bot pieces locked together in a rumble of crackly code. Was this the Codex's plan?

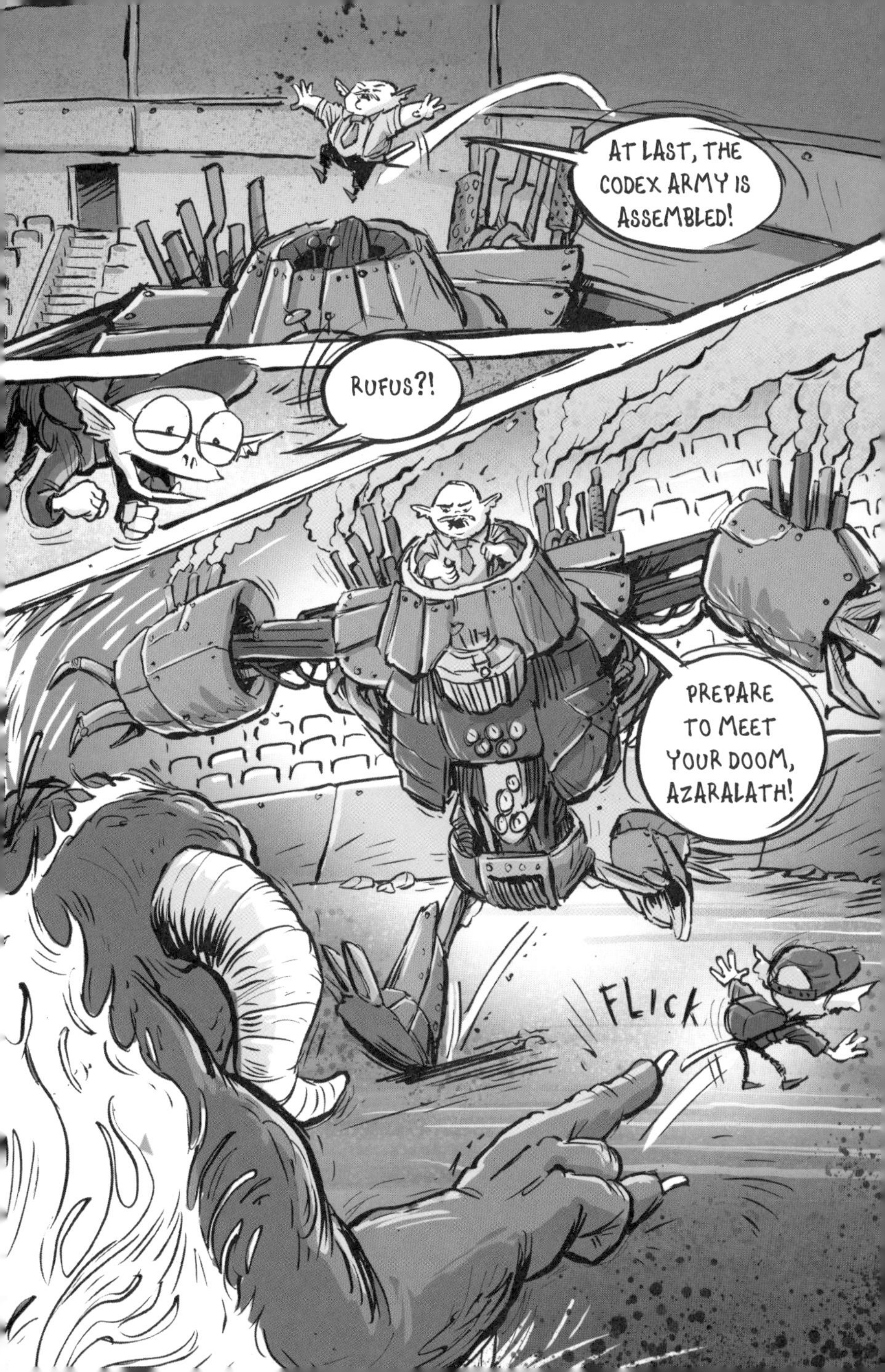
AT LAST, THE CODEX ARMY IS ASSEMBLED!
RUFUS?!
PREPARE TO MEET YOUR DOOM, AZARALATH!
FLICK

CHAPTER SEVENTEEN
Mega Bot Mash-Up

I hid under a pile of rubble, glad to be free from the demonic grip of Azaralath. Rizzo scrambled into the hiding spot beside me, elbowing me to make space.

"Out of the way, Fizzle!" he snarled.

I had never been so happy to hear the nickname I hated.

"Rizzo!" I said. "You saved me."

"Yeah, don't let it get around," he said. "I wasn't going to let that demon trash the whole city! Saving you was just a side effect."

A thunderous crash boomed above us as the Codex's Mega Battle Bot smashed the demon Az.

Rizzo nearly jumped out of his fur.

"That's enough heroics for me. Time to save my own tail. Later, Fizzle!"

Rizzo scrambled out from our hiding spot and ran across the arena on all fours. The battling titans were too busy locked in their struggle to notice the little kobold escape.

My own claws itched to follow him. It would be easy to slip away from this mess. Let the Codex's bot deal with Az the demon. That had been Rufus's plan all along. I had been too busy trying to stop the Codex from destroying Slick City to realize he was our only hope to save it. Time to get out of the way and let the big boys get the job done. I dug my claws into the dirt, ready to run.

A metallic crunch stopped me before I got started. The Codex's Mega Bot was down. Az loomed over the battle bot, ready to move in for the kill. Rufus frantically punched the controls of his bot. Each hit from the Mega Bot bounced harmlessly off the demon.

My tail corkscrewed with despair. Even the mighty Codex and his Mega Bot weren't enough to destroy Az. If the biggest battle bot in Rockfall Mountain couldn't win, what hope did the rest of us have?

And that's when I saw them.

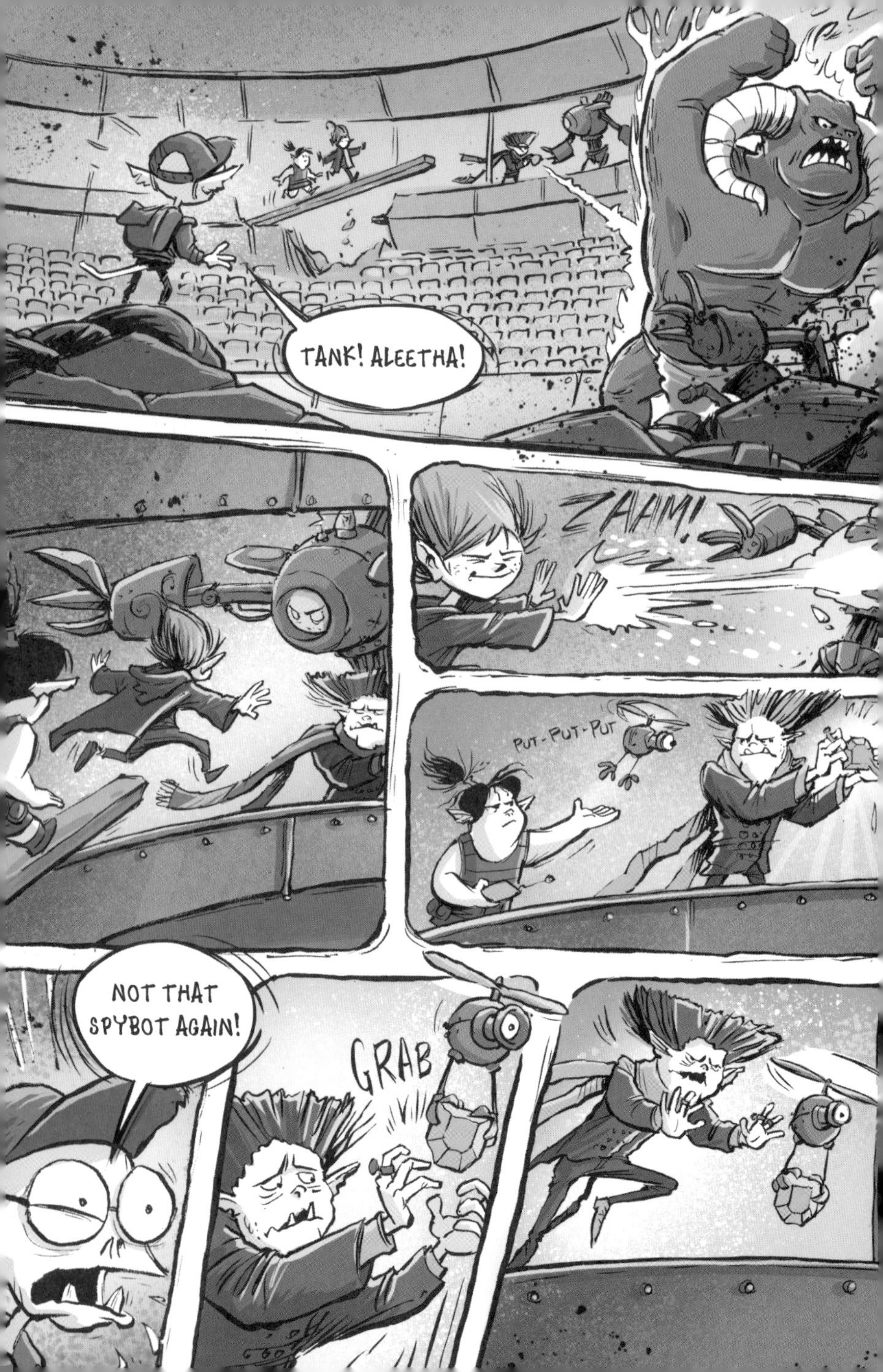
TANK! ALEETHA!
ZAAM!
PUT-PUT-PUT
NOT THAT SPYBOT AGAIN!
GRAB

I scrambled up the beam as fast as my claws could take me. I had to snatch Sanzin's flowstone before he grabbed it back. That stone let him control Az. If Sanzin didn't have the stone, he didn't have control.

I grabbed the jewel just as Sanzin got his balance on the beam.

"Hand it over, Fizz," Sanzin said. He wobbled on the narrow beam. Below us the massive flowstone swirled with purple light, like a whirlpool churning to another world.

The tiny flowstone felt heavy in my hand. It pulsed with ancient energy. A connection coursed through my body. A connection to a demon. I could feel Az's power run through me. I was connected to his mind.

I willed the demon to stop. And he did. I willed him to turn around. And he did.

I was controlling a demon.

Images of me showing up at school with old Az in tow ran through my brain. Rizzo's fur would fall out with fear. Weaver would never drag me into her office again. I could rule the school. I could rule Slick City!

Sanzin's eyes glowed with knowledge.

"You see what you are playing with, little goblin," he said. "The flowstone is too great a burden for someone your size. Give it to me. We can rule Slick City together."

Sanzin held out his long-fingered hand. The flowstone felt as heavy as a million math books. Handing it over to the troll would be much easier.

"Maybe you're right," I said. I didn't need a demon to stand up to Rizzo and his goons. I just needed to be me.

Sanzin smiled. "What a smart goblin you are."

"Smarter than you think."

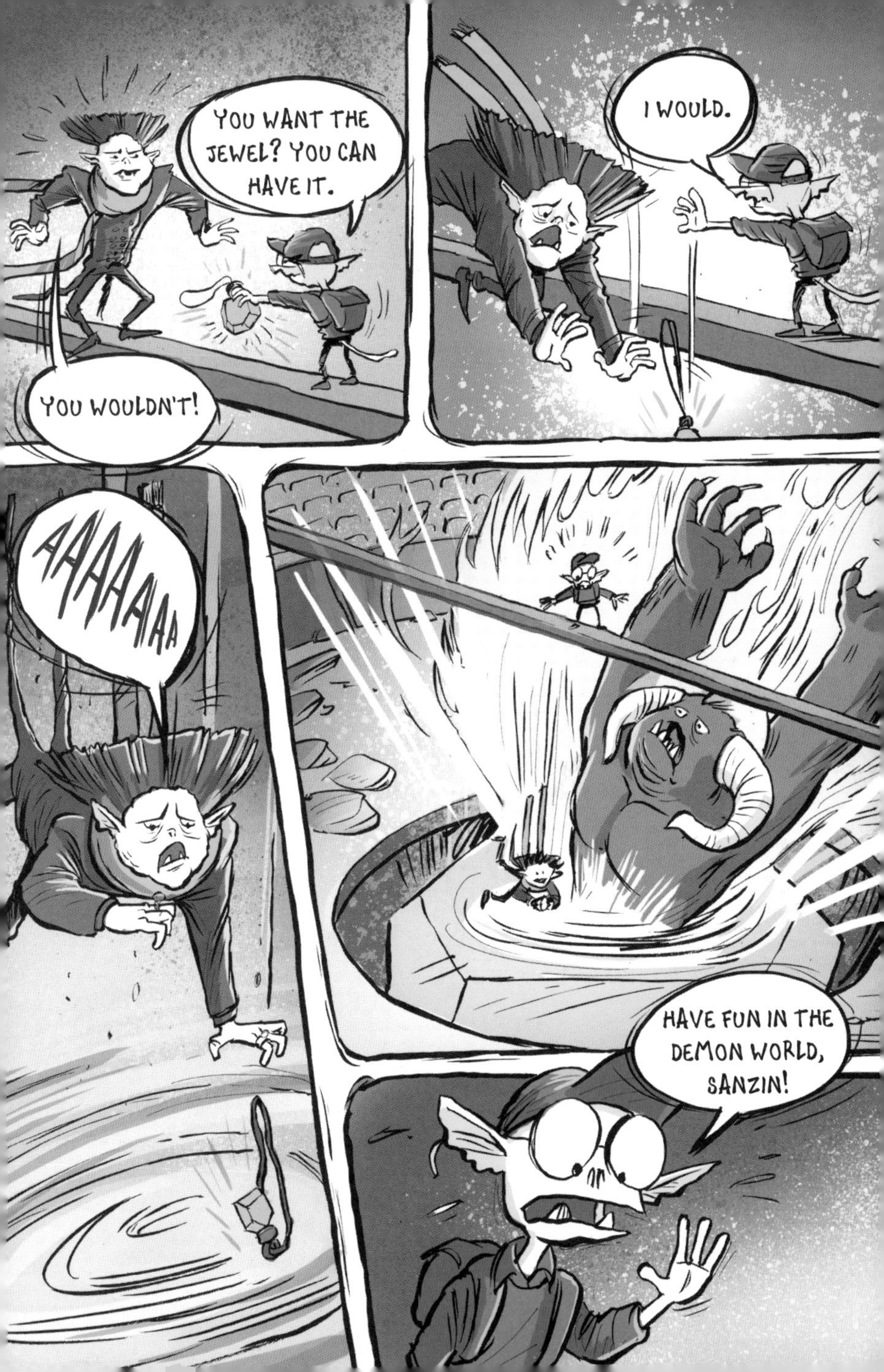
YOU WANT THE JEWEL? YOU CAN HAVE IT.
YOU WOULDN'T!
I WOULD.
AAAAAAAAA
HAVE FUN IN THE DEMON WORLD, SANZIN!

The best part about saving Slick City wasn't the medal we got from the mayor. It wasn't the big award ceremony at city hall, where my mom got to see me wear a tie. It wasn't even the season tickets to the Battle Bot League in the newly rebuilt and renamed Slick Stadium.

The best part of defeating a demon and saving the city was seeing Rizzo's face at school later that week.

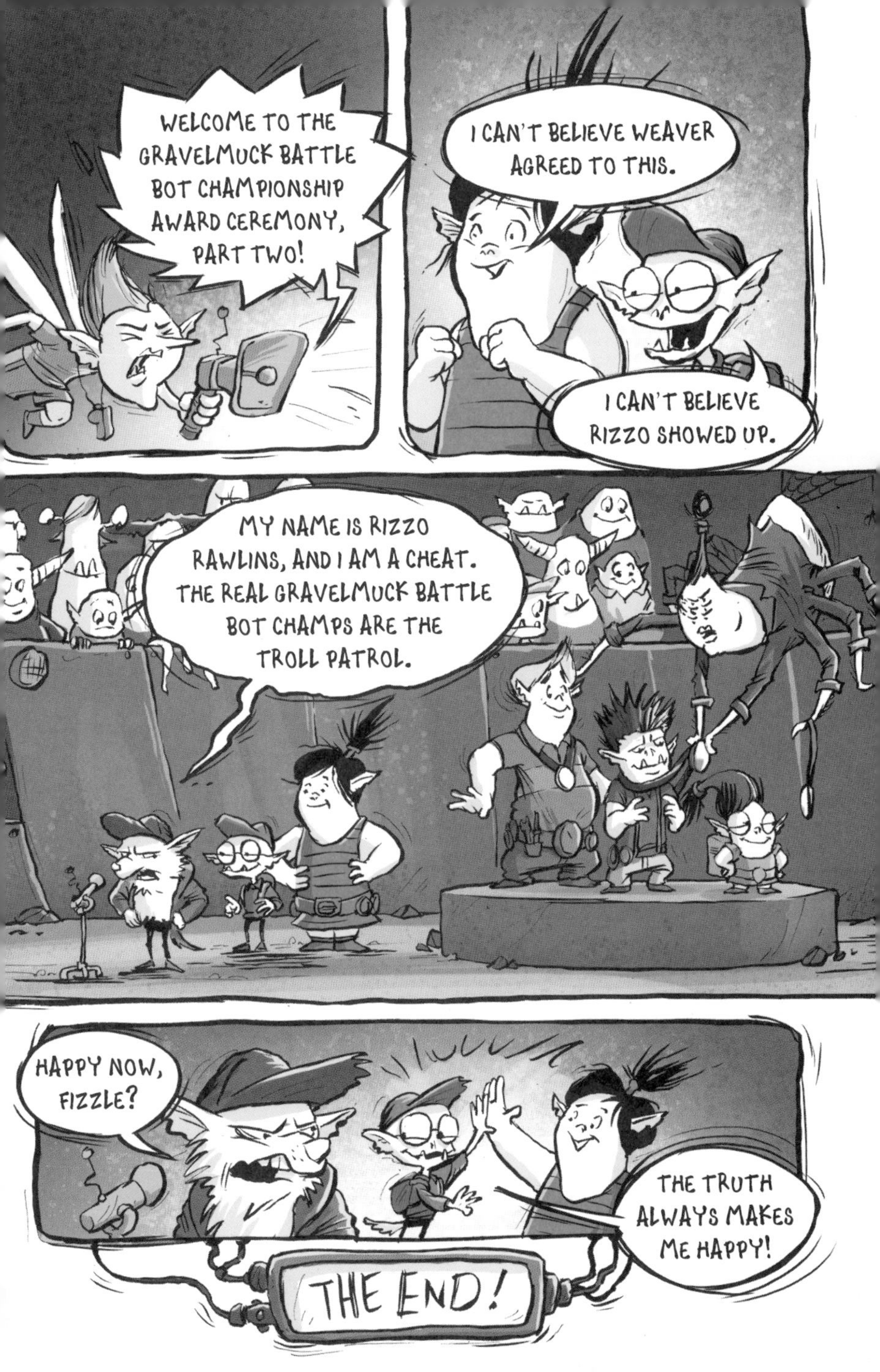
WELCOME TO THE GRAVELMUCK BATTLE BOT CHAMPIONSHIP AWARD CEREMONY, PART TWO!
I CAN'T BELIEVE WEAVER AGREED TO THIS.
I CAN'T BELIEVE RIZZO SHOWED UP.
MY NAME IS RIZZO RAWLINS, AND I AM A CHEAT. THE REAL GRAVELMUCK BATTLE BOT CHAMPS ARE THE TROLL PATROL.
HAPPY NOW, FIZZLE?
THE TRUTH ALWAYS MAKES ME HAPPY!
THE END!

LIAM O'DONNELL is an award-winning children's author and educator. He's created over thirty books for young readers, including the *Max Finder Mystery* and *Graphic Guide Adventure* series of graphic novels. Liam lives in Toronto, Ontario, where he divides his time between the computer and the coffeemaker. Visit him anytime at www.liamodonnell.com or follow him on Twitter @liamodonnell.

MIKE DEAS is an author/illustrator of graphic novels, including *Dalen and Gole* and the *Graphic Guide Adventure* series. While he grew up with a love of illustrative storytelling, Capilano College's Commercial Animation program helped Mike fine-tune his drawing skills and imagination. Mike and his wife, Nancy, currently live on Saltspring Island, British Columbia. For more information, visit www.deasillustration.com or follow him on Twitter @DeasIllos.

MORE GRAPHIC NOVELS FROM LIAM O'DONNELL AND MIKE DEAS

GRAPHIC GUIDE ADVENTURE SERIES

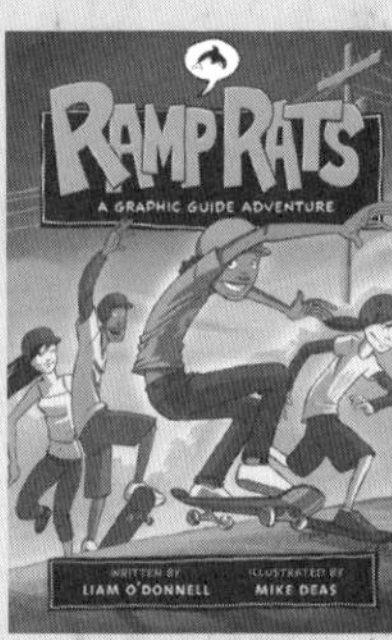
RAMP RATS
A GRAPHIC GUIDE ADVENTURE
WRITTEN BY
LIAM O'DONNELL
ILLUSTRATED BY
MIKE DEAS

9781551438801 • $9.95 PB

JUNIOR LIBRARY GUILD SELECTION

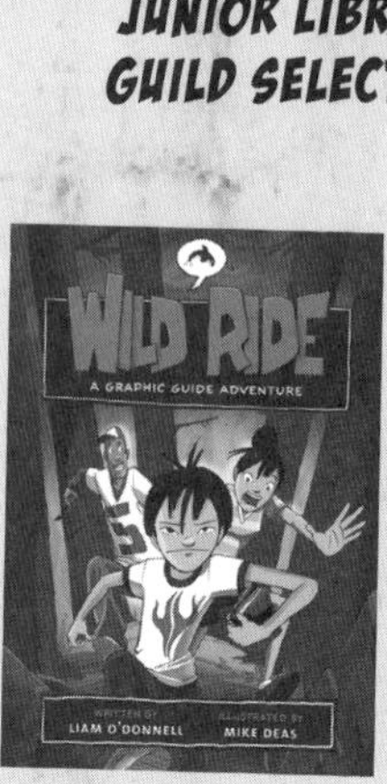
WILD RIDE
A GRAPHIC GUIDE ADVENTURE
WRITTEN BY
LIAM O'DONNELL
ILLUSTRATED BY
MIKE DEAS

9781551437569 • $9.95 PB

"Deas' illustrations are full of life."
—*Quill & Quire*

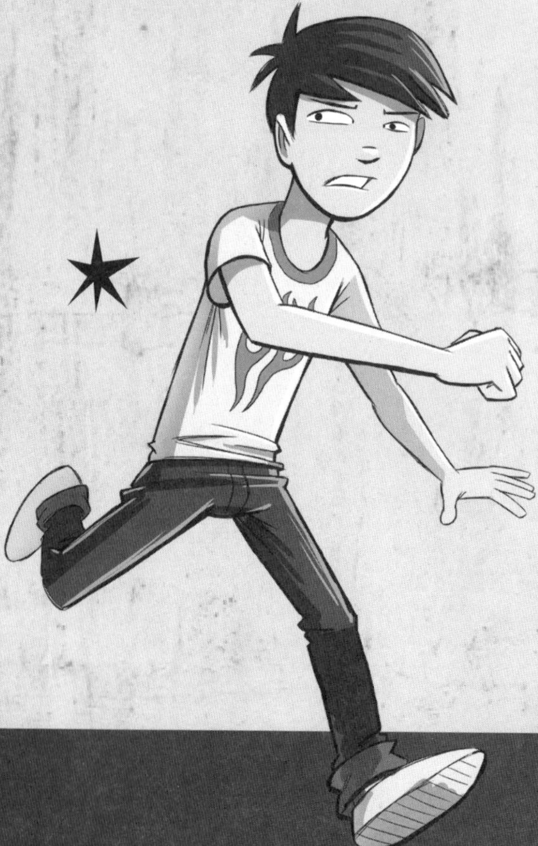

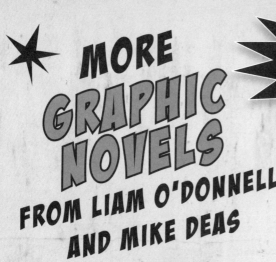

WHO LET THE SLIMES OUT?

Don't miss the first book in the Tank & Fizz mystery series!

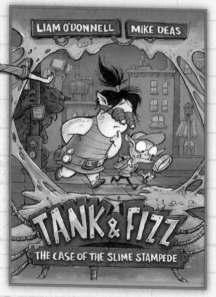

LIAM O'DONNELL   MIKE DEAS

TANK & FIZZ
THE CASE OF THE SLIME STAMPEDE

Tank & Fizz: The Case of the Slime Stampede
9781459808102 • $9.95 • Ages 8–11

The cleaning slimes have escaped, leaving a trail of acidic ooze throughout the schoolyard. Can detective duo Tank & Fizz solve this slimy mystery?

"Young readers will slurp up the gumshoes'
gooey first exploit with relish."
—*Kirkus Reviews*

"A monstrously imaginative and funny read."
—*Quill & Quire*

"Something slimy is running amuck in Rockfall
Mountains and it isn't the cleaning slimes. This
chapter book brims with reader appeal."
—*School Library Journal*

The adventures are
just beginning...
Watch for books
3 & 4

www.tankandfizz.com

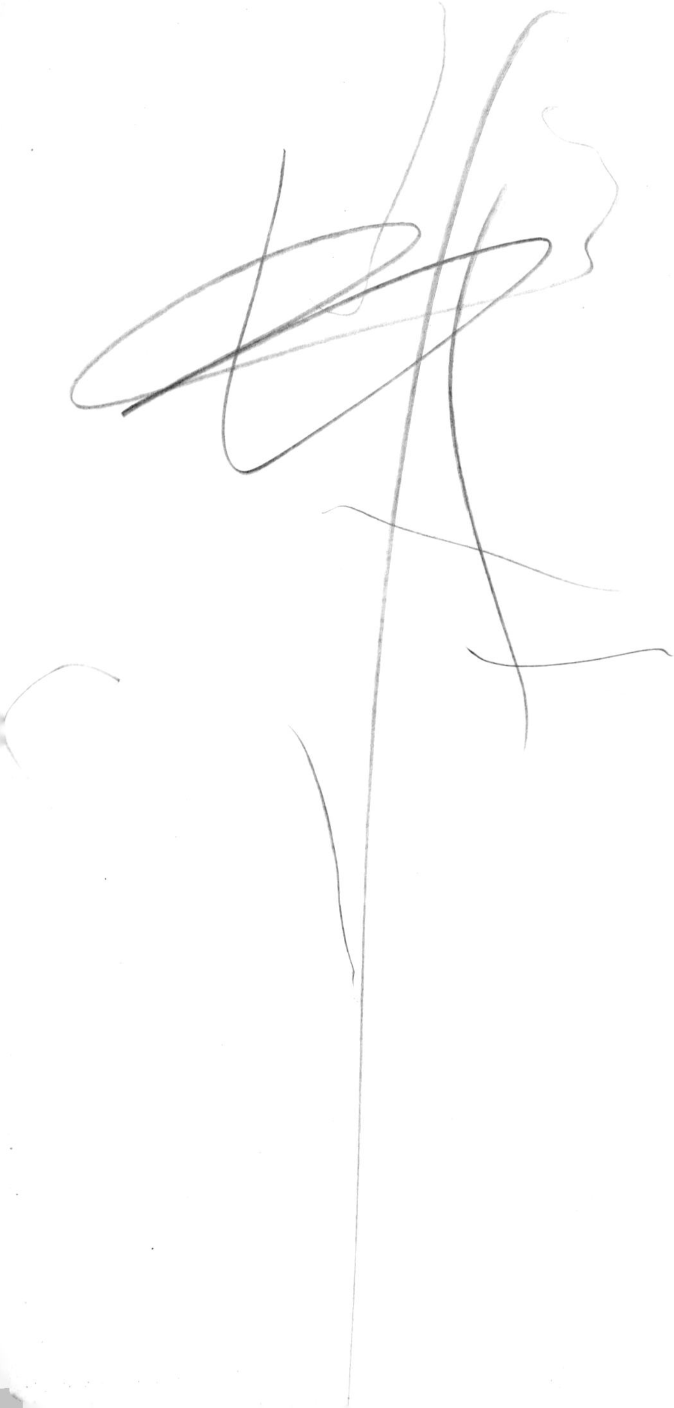